PRAISE FOR **FLINGS**

"At the root of Taylor's fiction is one of the great ineffable questions, so simple as to come off almost silly when stated plainly—why is the current state of things one way rather than another? Unanswerable, of course, but this collection cements Taylor's status as a young writer to follow." —*Daily Beast*

"Infused with pop-culture and literary references alike, Taylor's profoundly understated and often funny stories establish him as an unequivocal voice for the Internet age." —*Booklist*

"Taylor's insightful stories illuminate the many ways we fall in love—and out of it—and how romances shape our identity both while they last and long after they conclude."

—*Shelf Awareness*

"In this luminous collection of short stories, Taylor (*The Gospel of Anarchy*) takes on the theme of the constancy of self amid the ephemeral relationships that make up our lives. Academics and pizza-shop employees, the self-aware and the painfully deluded, a retiree, children at play in a Florida swimming pool—Taylor shows them all struggling with the daunting task of understanding love before it escapes them. The result is contemporary, intelligent, and occasionally laugh-out-loud funny. These stories, by turns witty and piercing, together form an uncommon portrait of the human heart."

—*Publi*̶ ̶ ̶ ̶ ̶ ̶iew)

"Taylor has created a coherent, fully inhabited world. . . . It's a book that demonstrates range by extending the author's skill with characterization and empathy to a broader range of voices and experiences, while at the same time remaining rooted in his earlier work's commitment to a scruffy, idiosyncratic brand of realism. If it were an ambitious third album by a Brit-pop band, it would be *Parklife*, not *Be Here Now*."

—Andrew Martin, *Brooklyn* magazine

"In style and content, Taylor's tightly crafted stories have been compared to a wide range of esteemed writers, including Raymond Carver, Denis Johnson, and Miranda July. . . . Though his characters may be aimless, Taylor retains a steely, self-serious control. . . . And his writing is refreshingly free of the smirk and snark that has come to nearly define contemporary fiction."

—*St. Louis Post-Dispatch*

"These are characters that surprised me when reading the book: the ways in which they come together, the ways in which they evolve, the ways in which they hold true to principles or abandon them or jettison elements of their life because of them. That blend of groundedness and unpredictability ultimately creates a fantastic sense of the unexpected in *Flings*."

—*Vol. 1 Brooklyn*

"Justin Taylor's *Flings* offers lasting pleasure."

—Elissa Schappell, *Vanity Fair*

"He's managed to gather up all the confusion, repressed aggression, and misplaced acceptance of growing up in the nineties and becoming a young adult in the twenty-first century. . . . But behind his contemporary premises, Taylor is practicing a brand of acute, oblique realism that stretches back to Carver and Yates and even to Sherwood Anderson, in which events act as triggers for memories that are the real story."

—Andrew Jimenez, *Paris Review*

"Justin Taylor's *Flings* is a great story collection, swoop[ing] through the world like a butterfly net capturing not only the way we speak but the way we think. . . . Justin Taylor has written an expansive collection of beauty, wisdom, and bigheartedness."

—Will Chancellor, *Bookforum*

"[Taylor] has mastered the art of funny/sad, and in doing so, his collection becomes a book as relatable as it is a fitting trademark of our modern lives."

—Heather Scott Partington, *Electric Literature*

"Taylor's messy worlds are . . . wonderfully endearing."

—*Interview*

"Taylor is equal parts hilarious and prescient, capable of finding the sublime in the most prosaic, diverse material."

—*The Millions*

"Justin Taylor's *Flings* is filled with stories both strikingly modern and perfectly structured, easily one of the year's finest short-fiction collections."

—Largehearted Boy, "Favorite Short Story Collections of 2014"

"Justin Taylor somehow makes available to us just how strange we are, here in late-capitalist early-twenty-first-century America. Taylor's stories chart a path through the truth, and the result is that *Flings* is urgent, necessary, funny, and amazing. A writer we need to read."   —Alexander Chee, author of *Edinburgh*

"The greatest books deepen our understanding of who we are, and *Flings* is one such magic text of anthropology. Taylor allows his characters a vulnerability that enchants and stings— these stories ache with truth, and their generative, smarting beauty rewards the reader with revelation time and time again. I tore through this book with white knuckles and a sense of relief, grateful to finally learn more about the human condition from an author who was willing to give it to me straight. Taylor is a brilliant writer who can tell it like it is without sacrificing style, humor, or surprise."

—Alissa Nutting, author of *Tampa*

"With such stylish and gut-bustingly funny sentences, and such a palpitant, beating heart, it is easy to overlook how serious and smart the stories in *Flings* are, arriving at one perfect ending after another. This is a book about people who strive for decency even as they rage against the warped and indecent rules of adulthood. Justin Taylor has been one of our best young writers for a while; with *Flings*, he takes a legit swing at major-league greatness."

—Charles Bock, author of *Beautiful Children*

"These stories capture the casual absurdity of everyday life while simultaneously illuminating the small, sacred miracles of friendship, compassion, and intimacy. Taylor's writing is sharp and confident, dark and potent. Every story in this superb collection rings with poignancy and oddity and sly, perverse pleasure." —Aryn Kyle, author of *The God of Animals*

FLINGS

FLINGS

STORIES

JUSTIN TAYLOR

HARPER ● PERENNIAL

NEW YORK ● LONDON ● TORONTO ● SYDNEY ● NEW DELHI ● AUCKLAND

HARPER ● PERENNIAL

A hardcover edition of this book was published in 2014 by HarperCollins Publishers.

HarperCollins books may be purchased for educational, business, or sales promotional use. For information please e-mail the Special Markets Department at SPsales@harpercollins.com.

These stories were first published—sometimes in different form—in the following publications: "Flings" in *Prairie Schooner*; "A Talking Cure" in *The Coffin Factory* and *Electric Literature's* Recommended Reading; "Adon Olam" in *Tweed's*; "After Ellen" in *The New Yorker*; "Poets" in *Five Chapters*; "Saint Wade" (as "Clark the Saint") in *Narrative*; "A Night Out" (as "Shot of Love") in *Brooklyn*; "The Happy Valley" in *Lucky Peach*; "Gregory's Year" in *Tablet*.

FIRST HARPER PERENNIAL EDITION PUBLISHED 2015.

Designed by Michael Correy

Library of Congress Cataloging-in-Publication Data has been applied for.

ISBN 978-0-06-231016-3 (pbk.)

15 16 17 18 19   OV/RRD   10 9 8 7 6 5 4 3 2 1

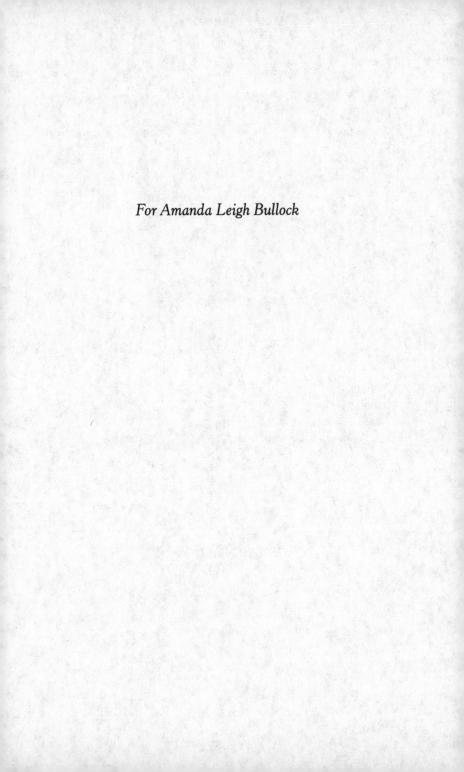

For Amanda Leigh Bullock

Rabbi Pinhas often cited the words: " 'A man's soul will teach him,' " and emphasized them by adding: "There is no man who is not incessantly being taught by his soul." One of his disciples asked: "If this is so, why don't men obey their souls?" "The soul teaches incessantly," Rabbi Pinhas explained, "but it never repeats."

—Martin Buber, *Tales of the Hasidim*

CONTENTS

CONTENTS

FLINGS

Percy took Intro to US Labor History for an elective in the spring of his sophomore year. The professor's name was Leon Pitzer, an embittered pinko genius with an august limp. In him Percy knew he had finally found the father surrogate he'd been searching for since arriving at Schmall, a semielite liberal arts college in a town of the same name in the heart of the heart of Ohio. Percy changed his major from English to history, and over the following three semesters took every course Pitzer offered. Pitzer directed Percy's senior thesis, an inspired treatise on the American government's illegal 1921 deployment of the Air Force to bomb striking mine workers at Blair Mountain, West Virginia. The SEIU invited Percy to come to Chicago and work on a hotel campaign. He talked to Kat about his decision. They both cried, but later, recounting the story to his best friend, Danny, on the porch over nightcap beers while Kat slept,

Percy tried to make it sound as if only Kat had cried. Danny knew the truth because his bedroom was across the hall from Kat's and he'd been listening in. "I don't get what the whole big deal is," he said to Rachel about it. "So he loves her, too. So what? Why is that some disaster? And what century does he live in where a man's not allowed to cry?"

"Are you, like, preparing me for something right now?" Rachel asked. She lived around the block from Danny. They were between her sheets and he held her tightly, as though the bed were a dinghy in some rough sea and he meant to keep her from going over. Rachel and their other friend Ellen—both film students—had managed to get their mentor to secure them internships working for an experimental West Coast filmmaker who staged an annual festival in Portland, Oregon. It was not clear when—or even whether—Danny and Rachel would see each other again. "Please don't say anything else," Rachel said. Danny clenched his jaw. Not talking when he felt like talking was pretty much the hardest thing in the world for him, and there were few people other than Rachel for whom he would do it. He thought of a popular song he'd hated in high school, the one with the chorus that went "Well, I guess *this* is growing up." He squeezed Rachel tighter, closer, begged her body to be his anchor, keep him from setting adrift in his own head. Nothing was going as anticipated. Her lower lip was between her front teeth. They enjoyed fast, rough sex and then she threw him out so she could shower and get dressed. She was due to meet her boyfriend, Marcus, for pizza. Instead of a good-bye kiss, or even a hug, they high-fived—a fierce flat sound that did not echo, and yet it rang in his ears the whole block home.

Danny knew he liked writing, and he knew he didn't want to move back to Kettering, and he knew he didn't want to stay in Schmall, especially not without his friends, but that was as much as he knew. So when a professor of his, presumably inspired by the STOP THE IMF! button on his backpack, offered to help him secure an internship at a prestigious-sounding New York political magazine that he had never heard of before, he told her he'd been a subscriber since he was fifteen and that it would be a dream come true. He printed out the application from their website and she wrote him a letter and the next thing he knew he was on a plane east.

His boss in New York had close-cropped hair and a permanent turtleneck: the arts and letters editor. One day they happened to return from their separate lunches at the same time and stood together in the low drone of the elevator. Danny ventured to comment that he was excited to see a new Branford Marsalis album coming out. He knew this because the editor had gotten a review copy in the mail earlier that day and, naturally, opening and sorting the editor's mail was one of Danny's several jobs. The editor brightened and asked if Danny was a fan, and Danny said, yes, he was. The editor asked what record Danny liked best and he said *Without a Net*, which the editor said he'd never heard of. Danny explained that it was a double live Grateful Dead record on which Marsalis sits in for a totally sick "Eyes of the World."

Let this anecdote serve as synecdoche for Danny's time in New York. Percy, meanwhile, had been relocated by the union to organize nursing homes all across Oregon state. He was moving to Portland, too! He took an apartment on Southeast Belmont Street in a low-rise building with open walkways across from a gourmet grocery store that he never once patronized. The first nursing home was in a town called La Grande, way out east in the Oregon desert—closer to Idaho than Portland. He lived in a motor lodge during the week and on Fridays drove the four hours back to the city. But for what? Nobody and nothing. Maybe drinks with Ellen and Rachel, if they were even around. He took his loneliness out on Kat, who was still back in Schmall. Not that he said it in so many words, but he was asking for her to come be with him. And who knew, Kat thought, but that maybe now they had a chance at the real thing.

So Kat sat around at the Belmont Street apartment while Percy was away all week organizing the nurses. He sent her lascivious promissory emails from his motel, and she responded in enthusiastic kind while IM-ing in a separate window with Danny in New York about his frustrations with the internship, her own boredom, and how despite everything it was honestly pretty cool. Gorgeous, cheap, progressive—the Great Northwest! Kat was looking for temp work. Once she had a job her days wouldn't be so empty and long. And once the La Grande home was organized Percy would ask the union to give him something closer to base so he could actually live in his apartment, and then they'd just see what they saw—wouldn't they? Danny supposed they would. "'Portland's a drawing card,'" Kat said, quoting that Raymond Carver story where the guy's wife sells vitamins while he sneaks around with her friend.

Rachel had asked Marcus to go with her to Portland, but he was unwilling to give up his "good job" at the hardware store in Schmall. She'd decided to live alone rather than share a place with Ellen and Ellen's boyfriend, Scott, a reasonably talented DJ with family money. It was assumed that Scott would soon propose to Ellen. He was balding, so his time seemed short, and it was understood among the friends that Ellen was bound to become famous like Miranda July. Ellen thought about how she'd phrase the Facebook update when the day came, or if instead she'd just post a picture of the ring on her finger, let the commentariat figure it out for themselves.

Rachel got a one-bedroom apartment on Couch Street— "couch" inexplicably pronounced "cooch" in the local demotic. She lived six blocks from Percy and Kat. The three ganged up on Danny about joining them. Percy and Kat said he could crash in their living room indefinitely; they had a futon. Rachel was notably silent on the subject of where Danny might live. Danny had fifteen hundred dollars in the bank. Since he wouldn't be paying rent the money would last him awhile, which meant he could devote himself entirely to two objectives: (1) write the great American novel, despite having never experienced anything of significance other than Rachel; (2) Rachel.

Danny, no sap like Kat, understood that he and Rachel would never be "together." And yet the allure of what they inflicted on each other—the sheer thrill of wounding and the deep satisfaction of licking each other's wounds clean—was too great to resist. He could not imagine living without it. He felt like he was waking from one of those dreams where when you're dreaming you think you're awake, and only when you wake up do you realize that what you thought was your waking life was in fact another tier of the big deep dream—or was it? Like Chuang Tzu and the butterfly, Danny thought to himself as the landing gear groaned and the plane began its descent into PDX. There was no such thing as New York. Danny saw that now. He wasn't one of Those People. He belonged to this strange town, his best friends. Her. Bedazzling, unaccountable girl who skipped the trip to the airport to meet his plane but turned up at the apartment at midnight for a late drink and to christen the futon after Percy and Kat went to bed.

So Danny's two projects were one and the same. Rachel was his muse—a word he no longer made the mistake of calling her to her face. Rachel hated to be written about. It made her feel like she was under some microscope, she said, or a zoo animal having its picture snapped by gawking tourists in foam hats. That made things difficult, though in a way it made them easier since he mostly only wrote out of anger, frustration, or hurt. For as often as she was bedding him, why didn't he matter more?

Ellen and Scott sublet a house in a suburb at the far edge of town. They went hard-core domestic and the other friends rarely saw them. Even Rachel only saw Ellen in passing at the filmmaker's office, where they were both rapidly learning the extent to which they had overestimated their interest in experimental film. Ellen seemed to take this in stride, but not Rachel. Impulsive and reckless at the best of times, in Portland she was rallying her disappointments into an all-out nihilism spree.

Rachel felt stuck, and neither she nor Danny was sure how Danny fit into the quagmire. Sometimes she clung to him: a nonjudgmental ear, the comforts of familiarity, and as much sloppy drunken sex as she could stand. He cherished these times and, though he did not know it consciously, was usually hoping for her to sink lower, because it was in her weakness that she called on him and he would once more have the chance to play the role of unwavering savior, at least until she got tired of having a savior, which never took all that long. She had come out there to find herself, but here was everything she'd left behind like a fence hemming her in or a bowline tying her to a dock. So she made friends with some townies in the music scene, which even she knew was a Band-Aid on a dog bite, but for the moment at least it would have to do.

While Rachel was out at house shows or watching kids in hoodies wipe out on their boards at the Burnside Skatepark, Danny sulked and wrote an endless, plotless book that was ostensibly dedicated to her but of which she was essentially the villain. Well, he had to work his feelings out somehow, didn't he? The only other choice would have been to talk to Percy about it, which he hated doing, because Percy related Danny and Rachel to him and Kat, and obviously in that formulation Danny was Kat. So he filled notebooks up with the grand tally of Rachel's misdeeds, transgressions, insensitivities, shortcomings, and general failure to sufficiently understand the grave importance of their love, which he regarded as a manifestation of capital-L Love in all of its philosophical, political, artistic, literary, existential, and metaphysical connotations and ramifications. Yes, whenever they made love the world was saved. He knew that, and so could hardly help but see that what they had was not a convenience, crutch, or habit but rather a solemn responsibility. It never once occurred to him that even if she'd understood the crazed scope of his vision, said vision still might not have been especially appealing to a girl adrift and unhappy in a world that she largely despised.

Rachel decided to do the stupidest thing she could think of, which was try heroin. Her townie friend Miles told her not to tell anyone about them going to shoot up, but she told Danny because she knew that he'd keep her secret, unlike Percy, who would tell Kat and then it would get back to Ellen, whose older brother had gotten bad into drugs in high school, resulting in a mess that had nearly torn her family apart. Nobody even smoked pot around Ellen. But Rachel knew she could trust Danny because she knew he would do absolutely anything for her except leave her alone. And this way, she reasoned to herself, he would feel nominally involved, despite the fact that he was absolutely not invited along. They were at the Cricket Cafe, a hipster diner whose specialty was biscuits and white gravy, though it was lunchtime now. The Velvet Underground happened to be on the house radio, and she hoped this coincidence somehow cli-chéd things to the point where he'd have to stop freaking out and laugh at the absurdity of it all—which he didn't, as she had known all along that he wouldn't.

Miles was going to handle the buy and getting clean works, as well as shooting her up and babysitting her. He knew what he was doing, she said; it was all taken care of. She wouldn't give Danny an address but grudgingly promised to keep her phone on.

Danny hated Miles. He was an unknown quantity, a dangerous usurper—everything, in short, that Danny had been to Marcus—though the few times Danny was allowed to meet him, Miles seemed nice enough. It was really only possible to hate him when he was an abstraction. The actual person just banged his head along with the music and asked if Danny wanted another beer. Miles was a high school dropout who played in a couple bands and had a three-year-old who lived not with him but with his parents, two towns over. He was doughy and soft-spoken, a moptop with hazel eyes and bad tattoos up and down his arms.

Ellen came home from work and found that Scott had left her. He'd loaded up their car with his half of their belongings, written a note about sad things sometimes being for the best, shut his phone off, and split. As Scott drove south he kept thinking that the cars passing him going the other direction were Percy on his way home, but that was because he only had the vaguest (and anyway mistaken) sense of where La Grande was on the map. He continued to entertain this possibility long after he crossed the California line.

When Ellen realized Scott was never going to pick up—and with Rachel MIA as well—she called Danny, who felt terrible having to pretend he didn't know why Rachel wasn't answering the phone. The world was wobbling on its axis. This wasn't supposed to happen. Ellen and Scott were supposed to have been the sure thing—the un-fucked-up and un-fuck-up-able couple, the golden standard against which the other friends could fail and fail absolutely, that task (he thought of Barthelme, who had been thinking of Beckett) standing always before them, like a meaning for their lives.

Ellen was alone out in the burbs, stuck with all the half-empty drawers and the craven, mealy-hearted note. Neither Kat nor Danny had a car with which to go retrieve her. Danny tried Percy, who was on the road home but still hours away. "Man, that sounds like an epic shit show," he said to Danny. "I've got half a mind to stay in La Grande." They shared a humorless laugh and then said good-bye. In the silence that followed, Percy considered the truth of what he'd said to Danny. It was a massive waste of time and money, all this travel back and forth, and there was a nurse named Jacquelyn with whom he'd become somewhat involved. If he turned back now he could get to her place by midnight, but then what would he say to his friends? Danny already knew he was on the way, so he'd have to make up an emergency. A union emergency? It didn't make sense. Percy's was the only car on the road. He imagined his headlights as streaking comets and his car as a dark ghost chasing their tails. That didn't make a ton of sense either but so what? Road signs flashed in and out of his vision. He didn't imagine himself at all.

Danny wanted Ellen to come to them, call a cab, but she was barely listening to what he said. There was no way she could wait patiently, give directions, sit back and watch streetlights roll by. She was in meltdown mode and someone had to get to her. Kat fired up the computer while Danny kept repeating, "It'll all be okay." Ellen hung up on him midsentence and he was suddenly worried that she might do something. The bus schedule was a nightmare—it was too late in the evening, there were too many transfers. Everything was wrong.

Danny called Rachel. Only he knew where she was, and she knew he knew; therefore if she saw it was him calling, she would know it was important because she would know that he would know that she'd kill him if he was calling her for no reason—or, worse yet, to check up.

Her phone rang, then went to voicemail. He wondered if she had broken her promise. He called again. The third time, finally, Miles picked up. Fucking Miles! "Hey, man," he said. Presumably he'd recognized Danny's name on her phone's little screen. Danny told him to put her on. "She's kinda . . ." he said, and then Danny started screaming at him. No idea what he was even saying. Miles told Danny to chill out and then he put the phone down. Danny heard voices, but he couldn't tell what was being said. A couple minutes passed.

Minutes. It was excruciating.

"What," she said, finally, in a blank voice that set Danny's guts churning. He launched into a garbled apology for having bothered her. "I'm hanging up," she said, but then before she could he blurted the news. "Oh no," she said, emotion seeping through the drug screen and into the two hushed syllables.

He wanted to apologize again but was scared to. Another epic silence.

"Okay," she said.

Half an hour later Rachel was banging on Ellen's door. Her nausea had mostly passed, but her hands were shaking. There was sweat on her forehead. She had chills. But they were there for each other. Ellen and Rachel forever! Friendship would carry the day where love had failed. Hours passed, crying and screaming, and then Ellen on the phone with her mother while Rachel—thrilled for the distraction—snuck outside and painted the rosebushes blue, a rejection of the Gatorade she'd chugged on the way over.

(Later, Rachel would tell Danny that Miles had gotten his hands on some seriously cheap shit. She'd drifted in a warm gray-on-gray la-la land for about twelve minutes; then the sickness had set in. Miles had called her to the phone from out of the bathroom, where she'd been huddled. All in all, she said, the biggest disappointment since the *Matrix* sequels.)

Danny sat slouched at Percy's kitchen table, swirling a wineglass full of Old Crow, his magnum opus splayed before him. His work was a disaster. He saw that now. His ostensible monument to Rachel was in reality a fairly astute but immensely boring exposition of his own most regrettable qualities and aggressive failures. His narrator was unreliable, unlikable, and calculating: a cipher for his worst self, a conniving sneak with a pornographer's eye for exploiting sentimentality, matched only by his penchant for producing actual pornography. Every sex act was recorded, but not as a memory or emblem of love; more like evidence entered into the record at a trial.

He finished the glass of bourbon and lurched about the apartment, flipping light switches off, closing shades.

The pioneer cemetery on Southeast 26th was a designated historical site, easily mistaken for a park and protected only by a chain-link fence. He hopped it, plunged headlong into the blizzard of shadows cast by the great oaks, silence booming like the sea in his ears. He realized that what the occasion required was music. Music consecrates everything and this was a holy moment, or it would be soon.

He picked a spot near—but not on—the grave of one Mollie Fletcher, 1832–1845. Poor kid. He piled the notebooks on the ground, then turned his attention to his iPod, a first-generation model about the size of a pack of cigarettes. He scrolled down to Rilo Kiley's *Take Offs and Landings* because Rachel had first turned him onto them, back three years ago when she'd been a bright-eyed indie rock girl. And because the first song on the album starts out "If you want to find yourself by traveling out West / Or if you want to find yourself somebody else that's better, go ahead." So it was pretty much perfect in every way. He turned the volume up as loud as it would go, knelt before his little pyre like Hendrix in that photo where his guitar's burning, hit the play button, stuck the device in the breast pocket of his plaid snap-button shirt. He coaxed a flame from his Zippo and held it to the pages of a spiral-bound Mead with a blue cover. It took. The cover curled up from its corner, revealing its white reverse side even as that whiteness blossomed into an orange that was already browning, the brown almost as quickly again becoming white-gray ash borne away on the breeze. He watched the fire take on a life of its own. Jenny Lewis's high, honeyed voice swarmed all the space between his ears, and everything she sang was the most important thing he had ever heard before, though he'd long known all these lines by heart. By the time he got to that song with the chorus that goes "These are times that can't be weathered and / We have never been back there since then," his great work was history and he was singing along with her. Cocooned in noise and self-pity, Danny felt like a pure spirit, righteous, the king of his own broken heart. He never heard the police approaching, or their shouts for him to get his goddamn hands in the air.

What could he have looked like to those night shift beat cops? A Satanist, perhaps: yowling on his knees before a fire in the old cemetery at close to the witching hour. His hands *were* in the air now, a lazy arrhythmic sway, but he still couldn't hear them, so they tasered him and he writhed on the ground in an ecstasy of suffering. His pants went piss-dark; the earphones flew free of his whipping head. From his new dirt-level vantage the wimpy fire looked scary and right. Then a second zap sent his eyes up into his skull.

Everyone came in the morning to bail him out. It was like the day he'd flown in, only Rachel was there, too, and everybody looked somber and fatigued. Danny was hungover, ashamed, rotten on Portland—fuck his court date; all he wanted was to leave town. They talked him down over breakfast at the Cricket—the same place he and Rachel had lunched the day before, lifetimes ago now. And what had the whole thing been about, anyway? He wouldn't say, only forked apart sopping pieces of the house special, his hand shaking as he raised it to his mouth. They let it go.

Not much changed between him and Rachel. They kept things status quo while her internship wound down; then she decided to go back to Schmall, not explicitly to get back together with Marcus but everyone knew it was in the cards. Percy's job moved him to Eugene and he didn't invite Kat along. She was bartending downtown and doing great for herself. She took over the lease at Rachel's place. Ellen got hired on at the film company but was just killing time. She wanted to go to law school, she thought.

Danny had a problem—he was homeless, almost broke, and needed to stick around town to finish his community service, or else live the rest of his life with a bench warrant out on him in the state of Oregon. He got a job doing shitwork for Greenpeace. Hey, you got a minute for the whales, the seals, the trees? He wore a blue windbreaker, held a brown clipboard, stood smack in the middle of the sidewalk. Ellen had more space than she knew what to do with out at her place and was glad for the company. She helped him buy a secondhand Trek bike to ride to work. It turned out that Danny and Ellen were the ones who were right for each other all along. Weird world. Weirder still for everything Ellen knew about Danny and Rachel, which was, well, everything.

They only had one secret from Ellen: the whole heroin saga, the third plotline of that already-storied April day—Danny and Rachel both gone dark with stupidity, and Ellen in her blazing grief. "You know what I think?" Rachel said to Danny one time. "There's nothing honorable about hurting someone you care about for no good reason. I think that the only way to make it up to her is to keep keeping the secret." They never brought it up again, even to each other. What else was there to say?

Ellen specialized in contract law at BU. Danny designed websites. They had a son and named him Dylan and were doing well for themselves but had no love for Boston, so when an opportunity arose in Hong Kong she said she wanted to take it. They lived in a tower in the Central Mid-Levels and Ellen commuted to an office in Taikoo. They had been in Asia nearly three years and loved it, but were always eager for their old friends to come visit. Rachel, freshly divorced at thirty-one from a man named Rowan, was encouraged and cajoled and prodded and finally said yes. She would come for thirteen days—all her vacation time, but the flight was fifteen hours so it hardly seemed worth it to come for less.

(Percy had died several years earlier, thrown from a horse while on a weekend getaway with Kat's successor. Kat herself still lived in Portland. She had a new set of friends, owned her apartment, sent e-cards on all their birthdays, but had basically written herself out of their lives.)

"I had the weirdest dream," Ellen says on the morning of the day Rachel lands. "I dreamed I never got tired of experimental film. I was on the faculty at Hampshire. I had this big brass key that opened a room full of old projectors. Also, I'd never quit smoking."

"I'm glad you quit smoking," Danny says. Then, "Have you ever even been to Hampshire?"

"I've never even been to Amherst," she says, laughing. They make love and then she has to get ready for work. She'd have liked to go with Danny to meet Rachel, but this whole week is going to be rough, in no small part because she's taking several personal days *next* week: they're going to show Rachel the city, do all that touristy stuff they're always hearing about but never seem to get around to checking out.

If you asked her, Ellen would say it is a testament to her own superlative taste in people that Danny and Rachel had the strength to exhaust their sickness for each other, then recover to achieve the chaste, sibling-like love they were always meant to enjoy. If this is a partisan reading, let it slide. Few enough stories end well, and even this one is haunted by the specter of Rachel's future, betrayed by but also bereft without that SOB Rowan. But that problem's on ice back in America, so for now let us say things are going well enough.

They drop Rachel's things at the apartment, then head right back out again: to Taikoo to meet Ellen for lunch. The trick is to stay busy so you stay awake. If you can make it through the first day, you'll sleep hard that night, beat your jet lag. Dylan's at kiddie gymnastics class with the live-in housekeeper, here called an amah, or helper. Ellen has to cut lunch short for a call. Danny and Rachel take the metro under the harbor to Kowloon, where they wander in and out of neighborhoods and markets until it gets dark. Ellen checks in via text every hour or so, but the upshot is she's not getting out of there anytime soon. Dylan's spent the whole day with the helper by this point, which Danny and Ellen agree is not to become a habit, but once in a blue moon like this won't damage his psyche irreparably, and the truth is even if they haul ass they won't make it home before bedtime. Danny could call the helper and tell her to keep Dylan up, but then they'll all pay tomorrow. Forget it, Ellen texts him back;

it'll be fine this one time. He agrees, signs off xoxoxo, and turns to Rachel, who's looking exhausted, so they head for the cross-harbor ferry, board, and find an empty bench on the upper deck where they sit, side by side, midway between two alien skylines on a small ship bobbing in the far-flung waves.

SUNGOLD

Twenty minutes max in the mushroom suit—that's the official rule. But it's still a smallish company and there are only two suits to share among twenty-one franchise locations, so there's pressure to make the most of your turn while it lasts. When the thirtieth franchise opens—late next year, if you believe HQ's projections—they say they'll order a third suit, and at fifty a fourth one, which sounds good until you realize that the proportion of mushroom suits to restaurants is actually in decline. Anyway, our turn started this morning and Ethan, that savvy entrepreneur, is eager to leverage this brand-growth opportunity, never mind that it's 95 degrees out with 100 percent humidity. He's a real trouper, Ethan. Especially since it's me in the suit and not him.

It's hard to stand upright in the suit, much less walk in it. I had to be led out here and planted on the corner where I'm sure to be seen by traffic in all directions. My own view, meanwhile, is like peering through the hair catch in a shower drain. "Wave your hands," Ethan advised me. "See if you can get people to honk."

Well, plenty of them do honk, but not because I'm waving my hands. The suit doesn't *have* hands. They're honking because the suit is bruise-purple, furry, and mottled with yellow amoebic forms across a cap like a stoner's idea of a wizard's hat blown up to the size of a golf umbrella, though I prefer to think of myself as a huge diseased alien cock. When sweat gets in my eyes I can't wipe them. The hair catch goes from HD to blurry. It's not that big of a switch.

Different people respond to the suit in different ways. Children stroke the fur, tug the cap if they can reach it. Then they ask it for presents. Their moms don't want them to touch it—"That's dirty, sweetie," they say, which is true, every square inch of it, inside and out—but they do want, inexplicably, for Junior to stand next to it—"Big smile now"—for a cell phone picture to text to Daddy, some guy in an office park scrolling through an emojis menu, looking for the one that says, *Why is our son standing in the shadow of a huge bruised dick?*

Frat boys throw a shoulder as they pass by, rarely bother to look back and witness my flailing attempts to stay on my feet. They know what flailing is; they've seen it. Their mandate is to induce, not to observe.

Bicyclists want me to get out of their way, which is not a realistic request given my ranges of speed and movement, but also, fuck them, they ought to be riding in the street. It's not my fault that's illegal in this backward-ass college town—though, having never ridden a bike myself, for all I know it's a Florida-wide thing. Anyway they scream at me. I would lunge *toward* them if I could lunge at all.

Black teenage boys—now this is interesting—will cross the street to avoid me. They'll sprint into traffic; I've seen it through the hair catch. And these are the same suave posses who practice their rhymes at full volume on the steps of the public library, who hit on girls from across the street. Now I'll grant you, a guy wearing a full-body fur mushroom suit to promote an organic vegetarian pizza pub is arguably the whitest thing to have occurred in the history of whiteness, but it's not as though it's going to rub off on them. It's not like it's contagious, like breathing the air around me will result in sudden loss of pigmentation, cravings for old *Friends* episodes, and, I don't know, a Dave Matthews box set. On the other hand, it's only fair to admit that *if* such a disease existed, and *if* it were airborne (as indeed mushroom spores are), then I am *exactly* the person who would be carrying it—patient zero, Typhoid Whitey—so maybe they're wise to play it safe.

Okay, you've got the picture: this is a shitty job. But not everything about it's shitty. In fact there are many perks. I'll tell you.

First, I get paid under the table. As far as the federal government's concerned, I haven't earned a taxable dime in three years. Second, I get a free shift meal every day I work, plus whatever I can steal, which is plenty. I mean it's not just food and booze. Ethan is a terrible businessman, the worst I've ever encountered: a blackout alcoholic and probably bipolar, though he's also a cokehead and smokehound, so maybe his emotional swerves are side effects—or, rather, the intended effects—of the way he paces his days. What I'm trying to put across here is that Ethan's the perfect boss. He is reason number three or, really, all the reasons. Whenever I see a light on in the restaurant after hours, I knock on the kitchen window, find him rolling blunts at the salad station or deep-throating the spigot on the Jagerator, a medium quattro formaggi in the oven and him without anyone to share it with. He unlocks the back door for me, and forty-five minutes later I'm shit-faced, fed, and getting another raise.

Ethan is a self-sabotaging trust fund maniac whose folks set him up with this franchise for his thirtieth birthday, mostly, I think, so he'd have somewhere other than the grounds of the family estate—a former plantation, it could have gone without saying—to play "In Memory of Elizabeth Reed" at blowout volume a dozen times a day. As long as he keeps his annual losses in the mid five figures they'll keep him in business. So he has his clubhouse—with its audiophile-grade sound system, bulk alcohol purchase orders, and Showtime After Dark–grade waitstaff—and the family is spared both the Allman Brothers and the train wreck, if that's not too redundant to say. The college, for its part, inducts a freshman class every single year. (I myself was in it once, and look at me now!)

These kids, like I did, come from towns where the vegetable on the menu—when there is one—is either Jell-O or tuna fish salad, so organic mozzarella cheese is a legitimate thrill.

The girls we hire cut deep Vs into the necks of their uniform tie-dye T-shirts, which is technically a violation of the terms of our franchise agreement, but so far nobody's complained. I don't know who started this tradition. I also don't know why an eighteen-year-old girl—a girl who's been in town all of four days; who decides to try our restaurant for lunch because there was a 20-percent-off coupon in her dormitory welcome packet and we're on the only off-campus street she can name; who walks over here, comes in, sits down, has to shout over the strains of "Melissa" or "Jessica" to give her order to a server who for her part is probably *named* Melissa or Jessica, wearing tell-all jeans shorts and a shirt that's essentially confetti; who is charged $8.95 for two pieces of pizza and a Sprite (that's *with* the coupon, mind you, and before tip)—stands up at the end of her dining experience, brushes the cornmeal off her skirt, and thinks to herself, *How do I become the slut who just served me lunch?* But it happens, man. It happens like clockwork, and the lesson—not the first or the last time I've learned it—is that there's an awful lot of shit in this world that I don't know.

Ethan hires girls he wants to fuck, obviously. I mean he hires girls everybody wants to fuck: radiant vortices of bleach, wax, and puka shells who know exactly what you're thinking when you look at them, who sound like TV shows—believe me— when they're pretending to get off. To Ethan's credit—and this is the only time you'll catch me using that turn of phrase—he doesn't fire them for not fucking him. He waits until he catches them stealing; *then* he fires them. And they always end up stealing, irrespective of whether they need the money. Need's got nothing to do with it. Ethan's just a hard guy not to steal from. He brings something out in people. I'm lucky he doesn't want to fuck me because it keeps him from noticing how badly I'm fucking him. If I had tits I'd have been shit-canned years ago. Instead I keep getting promoted, to the point where I've become a kind of imperial factotum, body man for the restaurant, what in a real place of business would likely be described as "the manager," a term Ethan abjures on account of its lack of good vibes. I do the books and the purchase orders, the scheduling, plus incidental waiting, bussing, onion chopping, secret sauce mixing (half balsamic vinegar, half anchovy-free Caesar dressing, pinch of salt), and of course, at the moment, I wear the mushroom suit. It's some low-down proletarian shit, I'll grant you, especially for a guy closer in age to Ethan than the Melissa/Jessicas, but you know what? I've got an ex who adjuncts at the college and I know what she makes per poetry workshop. I also know what her current squeeze—a math PhD—gets for his Intro Stat lecture, a class that seats four hundred and is simulcast on the web to twice as many again. I'll own a house before those motherfuckers, that's for sure.

A light goes out and then comes on again, but it's blurry—I mean blurrier than usual. I feel oddly relaxed but also weighed down somehow . . . somehow . . .

Oh, that's right.

The suit seems to have become horizontal, and me with it, and there seems to be a transition scene missing, so smart money says I had a bit of heatstroke and fainted, fell. I'm facing upright—that blurry light would seem to be the sky—but stuck. If it rained right now I'd drown, which is scary, but somehow not scary enough to keep me from blacking back out.

Light again, and a dark shape blocking most of it, but a light-dark shape if that makes any sense, and long, thin golden strands descending through the grille mesh, tickling my nose. That's hair. (And so much then for the hair catch analogy.) The strands belong to one of our newer Melissa/Jessicas, who must have looked out the front window and noticed that a certain purple obscenity had dropped out of the landscape. Already proving herself a team player, this Melissa/Jessica. I ought to learn her real name, would ask her except I should probably already know it: there's a good chance Ethan told me, or that she herself has, possibly when I interviewed and hired her, which it's entirely possible I'm the one who did.

"Hey," she says. "Let me help you." As if I could stop her; as if she could help. But I don't say anything. Let her tug and jostle me a while; the sooner she tires herself out, the sooner she'll go get Ethan. Even through the stink of this suit, I can smell her: whatever lotion she uses, coconut-y, and beneath that a hint of something danker, the smell of her futile exertion, maybe, though I may be smelling myself.

My nose still tickles. I'm holding back a sneeze, and then all of a sudden I'm losing hold, have lost it, am making a noise that's half donkey bray and half kicked cat. My whole body shudders with the force of it, snot all over my face, the suit rocking slightly from side to side on the metal hoop sewn beneath the fur of the mushroom cap's rim.

The good news is that observing this physics lesson seems to have given Melissa/Jessica an idea. "I've like totally got this," she says, and rolls me over on my rim so I'm facing downward, suspended two feet above the earth, watching ants march across the concrete in my shadow while gravity, happily, works some of this snot off my face. Melissa/Jessica digs around in the fur of the mushroom stem, searching for the industrial-gauge zipper, which is located exactly where I'd never be able to reach it even if the suit had arms. She unzips me in one long quick pull, like it's prom night and she's me and I'm the best she could get.

With my newly expanded range of motion I wriggle an arm free, wipe my face off with my hand, wipe my hand off on the grille mesh, then stand up and step out. The suit is splayed open on the ground like a butchered animal, a husked chrysalis, an egg sac from which I'm emerging, a born or reborn creature, baffled by the sunlight, covered head to toe in slime.

(When you go steady with a poetry prof for as long as I did, you can't help learning a few things about poetry, so don't go getting incredulous—or, worse yet, impressed—that I talk so much less dumb than I live.)

We can't leave the suit where it's fallen, so I throw my arms around its dead weight, heave, and lift. It's not especially heavy— thirty pounds at a guess, maybe forty—or difficult to maneuver, provided of course that you aren't straitjacketed inside it.

I come back inside with the suit in a fireman's carry, having refused Melissa/Jessica's offers of assistance (and also having failed to learn or relearn her name). I march it right through the dining room and the kitchen, on back to the supply closet. I drop it on the floor in the corner, give it a few kicks and a stream of curses, and when I turn around she's standing there holding a large Sprite with extra ice in one hand and a clean shirt in the other. The shirt is a size too small and has already had its neck V'd. "All I could find," she says.

"Where the fuck is Ethan?"

"Haven't seen him."

Deep breaths. I'm taking deep breaths. First in for three whole seconds, then three seconds of stillness, then three seconds to exhale. I had planned to end this day with another raise for what I've been through, but the experience will be worthless in the retelling; it will sound like mere slapstick to Ethan, and that's assuming he's able to follow the plot.

I take my shirt off and drop-kick it toward the mushroom suit, pick a dishrag from the reserve stash we keep back here, start to wipe myself dry. She watches me do all this, following the movement of the cloth up and down my body with her eyes. Well, why not? I've got good definition. My momentary weakness in the preceding episode was strictly the product of circumstance, the heat index and smothering getup. In the normal course of things I set an example of *rude health* in the enviable young-Whitmanic sense. What I mean is, it's no surprise that this chick's scoping me, even though my hair gel evaporated while I was frying in the suit.

When I'm clean and crammed into the new shirt, I look at her and see she's still looking. "This is for you, too," she says, handing me the Sprite. Then she mumbles something about needing to get back out on the floor, which is understandable. This fiasco's been unfolding for half an hour already, and the girl works for tips.

I drink half the Sprite, then pour Svedka into the cup until it's full again, the logic being that if I'm stuck dressed like a sorority girl at a Phish show then I might as well drink like one. Four o'clock hits, which means it's shift change, also time to switch out the register, get the lunch take counted and into the safe. Still no sign of Ethan, which doesn't surprise me. He likes his restaurant much better when it's closed.

I plant myself at the front bar with my supersize cocktail, wish a good day to one and all Melissa/Jessicas as they clock out. Most can't seem to get their gazes above my V-neck—my chest hair like a squirrel in the jaws of a rainbow, which is something to see, I guess. I put a new drawer in the register, put the lunch drawer up on the bar in front of me, and set out to do the skim before I'm too bombed to count. I use a very sophisticated system. First I count up all the money; then I imagine what Ethan's likely to expect the take to have been, and from there ballpark what he's likely to notice missing. Then I remind myself who I'm dealing with and double the figure, plus another forty bucks for my trouble. Then I count it again to be sure.

I'm almost finished when I notice someone standing nearby. Not looming, exactly, but decidedly in my space. My first thought is I'm about to get robbed, and that I deserve it, sitting out here like an asshole with these stacks of money. But when I bother to look up, I see it's not a robber but rather a girl, albeit not the kind we're used to seeing in here. She's got a helmet of thick curly hair and a truck-like bearing, is wearing black slacks and a chambray button-up, long sleeves in *this* fucking weather, which explains the sweat on her brow, lip, and neck. I'm not going to stand up because if I do she'll know she's taller than I am. Not a lot taller, but taller.

"Hi," she says in what sounds like a best-guess imitation of perkiness, as if she's been watching all day through the windows, trying to figure out what the Melissa/Jessicas sound like based on the way they walk. "Do you have any openings? I brought a résumé." She holds out a paper that I don't take from her. Her name is centered in bold letters at the top of it, followed by email address, phone number, and grade point average. Below that the page is inkless, a tundra.

"Appolinaria Pavlovna Sungold," I say. "You're shitting me."

She shrugs. "Most people call me Polina."

"I think I'll call you Sungold."

She shrugs again. "Does this mean I'm hired?"

"Hang on a sec there, Sungold. Okay. This place has a certain kind of, uh, vibe. Do you know what a vibe is? How sometimes you're somewhere and it's like things seem to mystically vibrate in a certain way? Don't answer that. But look around you. Look at the other waitresses, the stuff on the walls. Look at *me*, for God's sake, this thing I'm wearing as a shirt."

"You mean your shirt?"

"Right. I am wearing what is worn here. By the girls, I mean. I don't wear this usually, but today is special. I guess what I'm trying to say is, when you look around, does this feel like your wavelength? Can you see yourself vibrating here?"

"I could wear the shirt the way it comes, without cutting it."

"Not on your life, sister. The guy who owns this place? Forget it. Not on your life and certainly not on mine."

But you know what? I'm starting to like this Sungold. And now that I've mentioned Ethan I'm picturing his disappointment, not to mention the stifled confusion on Melissa/Jessica's collective face. Then Sungold says the thing that seals it, what amounts to the magic words: "I can tell what you're doing with the money. For ten percent of whatever you're taking I'll not only help you but I won't rat you out."

Ten percent! Jesus, that's decency. Downright chivalrous. I count her share out on the spot.

But the sexy T-shirt thing is a problem, one I worry may prove intractable until I see Sungold's solution. She lays her ladies' XL out on a cutting board in the back. The sleeves go first, then the hem; the neck plunges; a diamond cutout pattern blossoms up the sides. She slips it on over her chambray and asks me to show her around.

She comes to work every day like this, and while it doesn't do her bearing (or her sweating) any favors, she never messes up an order or lets a plate sit in the kitchen, so between the occasional pity tip and what we're stealing she more than makes up for what she loses not showing her tits off, for having tits no one wants to see.

As predicted—as counted on—Ethan hates her. He says she compromises brand integrity, but I stand firm. It's important, I tell him, to have at least one other person around who can lift a box of bread dough or the ten-gallon bucket of feta cheese. It's not as if he's going to carry these things himself. Sungold could wear the mushroom suit, too, I bet, though I never suggest it, and Ethan has the memory of an infant or a goldfish, which is why he's such a shitty capitalist and such an amazing boss. The suit lies fermenting in the supply closet, forgotten until HQ calls with the address of the store we're supposed to pass it on to, a newish franchise in another college town—Valdosta, Georgia, some hundred miles north of here, give or take. So here I am, wrangling its rancid, still-damp, mold-fluoresced corpse into the back of my truck.

"Take this for gas, man," says Ethan, little thicket of bills between two fingers like a stubbed-out cigar. "Get lunch or whatever. I appreciate you doing this. There's a show at Side Bar tonight that I'd seriously die if I missed it. You ever heard of the Flower Rangers? Killer. You should check 'em out." My God but he's a sorry sight in daylight: crow's-feet and gin blossoms, scabby eczemas at the hairline, neck tripled up on itself in blood-flushed rolls. He looks like he might die *at* the concert, or maybe on the way to the venue, or maybe right here while we're talking if I don't hurry up.

I take his money, tell him he's more than welcome, that it's my pleasure. "Have fun tonight, Ethan. Get your dick sucked for me."

"Sure thing," he says, though we both know he won't.

Sungold's in my shotgun seat, rolling us cigarettes. The second part of this favor is I have to bring her with me. Ethan was adamant. I pretended first to resist, then to relent.

Sungold isn't her original last name, obviously—I mean *historically*—though it is the name that she was born with. Her father picked it out not long after he came over as a strapping young bootstrapper in the early '80s. He saw it printed on the side of a box of tomatoes in a grocery store and thought it sounded American, Floridian, full of hope: sun and gold. It wasn't until he had a daughter that he got sentimental, nostalgic for the homeland and patronymics. Her three older brothers are named Franklin, Reagan, and Henry Ford.

She's telling me this while we're driving through the void that Florida becomes outside of all city limits (and sometimes within them). I tell her she's lucky he didn't spot an Ovengold turkey in the deli case, or a roadside stand selling sunchokes or, worse yet, boiled peanuts. "Although boiled peanuts are pretty awesome. Holler if you see a sign. We'll stop."

She gets the Cajun flavor and I get original recipe, the kind that taste like hot, slippery salt. Then the sky opens up with a thunderclap, unleashes white blinding curtains of rain that at first I think we should power through, try to get on the other side of, but after we're passed by a big rig that was invisible until the moment it boomed by us, I decide to pull over, wait it out. We taste each other's peanuts and talk about music, specifically how much we hate Ethan's taste in it. She says she likes hip-hop, mostly, but also Joni Mitchell and the Kinks. I like hip-hop, too, but for some reason scroll past Jay Z and Kanye to find the most esoteric thing in my arsenal, this Royal Trux album where they sound like the Rolling Stones in a blender full of heroin—one of the poetry prof's touchstones, as if that needed to be said. The poetry prof once told me that for people who think Stephen Malkmus is Jesus, the Royal Trux are like the Old Testament. I didn't tell her that I didn't know—or care—who Stephen Malkmus was, and she chose to interpret my silence as contemplative pleasure (our signature form of miscommunication) so she Dropboxed me the MP3s, which got cloud-backupped to my phone the last time I updated, but I guess I'm the one who never deleted the album. I have no idea what I want Sungold to think of it, or of me for having chosen to put it on. In the rearview mirror I can see the mushroom suit getting ruined in the truck bed while we fill the cabin with American Spirit smoke and try to relate to these schedule-one ballads—if they are ballads—which come to think of it make more sense right now than they ever have before. They're the perfect sound track to this obliterating rain.

I want to revise something I said earlier, the thing about nobody wanting to see Sungold's tits. I want to see them. I think she wears a sports bra beneath her chambray, holding back great sloppy fat ones, and I want to take them across the face. She's easy to be around and smart, and I like the sound of her voice, apart from whatever it is she's talking about, though increasingly

I find myself attending to the actual words she says. I hired her as a joke on Ethan, and now I feel awful about it, but also grateful to get to have her around all the time, which in turn makes me feel both better and worse. No more salacious idolatry of Melissa/Jessica—that honey trap, that photo spread. I want to fuck Sungold till she prays in her mother tongue. I want to suck my own come off the tip of her clitoris. I want to love her everywhere she stinks from and give her half of everything I steal.

I start telling all this to Sungold but somehow it comes out wrong. She gets hung up on the preface to my conversion, doesn't like my summary judgment of Melissa/Jessica, is offended on their behalf and never mind the fact that their mere existence has made her own life more difficult in a thousand ways—though I should admit that this is a fact whose facticity she disputes. I probably shouldn't have mentioned her clit at all.

Sungold has this idea that women are to be respected irrespective of who they are and what they look (or smell) like—that is, for no reason. She says I talk about women like they're some exotic species of animal, as though hunt-and-capture were the only mode of interaction, as if their bodies were a personal provocation, as though their lives were an aspect of my life rather than self-contained, inviolable, requiring no justification, and lived without reference to me.

For a minute it seems like we're finally understanding each other. I start to get excited again. A minute later this turns out to have been premature. Simply to understand a position is not to endorse it, apparently. Her disgust is palpable, material, feels as real as the rain on the windshield or the mud we discover we're stuck in when I try to put the truck back on the road.

"What now?" I say and she looks at me in this way that says, *I am babysitting a tiresome and probably retarded child.* It's the same look I give Ethan whenever he's not looking at me.

"We push," she says, and opens the truck door, hops out, hits the mud with a squelch.

The mushroom suit's pulp by the time we get it to the restaurant. The manager meets us in the parking lot, unhappy. He's got facial hair that tells you he knows how to use all the alternate heads his electric razor came with, that he's paid for more than one Baptist girl's abortion but still votes Republican because he expects to retire rich. He can see we're muddy but he doesn't offer us use of his facilities. He doesn't even offer us to-go cups. We are obviously the worst thing that has happened to him all month.

Through the front windows we can see that here the servers' shirts have not been cut to pornographic ribbons. They wear 501s and arch-supportive closed-toe shoes; a range of genders, age brackets, and body types are represented among their ranks. Still not a black person to be seen anywhere, but of course there are miracles and then there are miracles. As the busboys unload the carcass we can hear jazz at a civilized decibel. It's probably a miserable place to work. I bet they notice if you steal.

"Thanks for the hospitality," I say to the manager.

"Thanks for nothing," he says and smacks the truck gate, as if we needed another clue that it's time to leave.

• • •

I use the drive home to walk back the worst of what I said during my epiphany. "I'm not unteachable," I tell Polina. "My worldview could stand some realignment, sure."

"I'm not your teacher," she says. "I'm your employee, your accessory to fraud, and your friend, kind of, or I was until you decided my mouth would look better with your dick in it, which by the way is the reason that me and the other waitresses are more the same than different, why we have solidarity—or ought to have it—even if they are a nasty bunch of anorexic airhead cunts."

Startled, I take my eyes off the road and look over, find her smiling shyly in the passenger seat, two fresh smokes rolled up and ready to go.

"You *are* my teacher," I say. "A magic Russo American sent to my life to make it better—to make *me* better. But your life is also a life. I see that now. I'm going to make your life better, somehow."

"Fifty percent would be better."

"I wasn't sure if you'd remember I said that," I say. "I mean it was mixed in with all that other stuff that made you mad."

"How about it's the only thing I remember?"

"Thank you."

"You're welcome."

"I liked the way you said 'solidarity' before. It sounded very Russian."

"I say it the way my father says it. I like to say it's the only Russian word I know."

"Would you say it again for me?"

"*Solidarity.*" We smile at each other. She pauses a moment. I can hear her teeth grind while she thinks about something. Time passes—not a long time, but time. I keep my eyes roadward, high beams burning away the darkness, bleaching the trees. "It was nice," she says, finally. "The thing you said about my clit. Don't get me wrong, you shouldn't have said it, and you're never going to do it, but it was nice to hear."

Early the next week the letters start coming from HQ. No more phone calls. They want records now, a paper trail. The restaurant is billed for a new mushroom suit. Apparently there's a reason they don't have a hundred of those things in a warehouse somewhere, and now I know what that reason is. Plus, we learn, HQ has been sending secret shoppers in here, and the reports have not been good. We're drowning in violations. Our Caesar dressing tests positive for anchovies. We are beyond probation. The choice is between closing our doors immediately and getting sued to death.

"I'm so fucked," Ethan says, drunk as I've ever seen him but sounding scarily sober. I pull the lever on the Jagerator, top us both off (and I should, or maybe shouldn't, specify that we're drinking out of pint glasses).

"You're not fucked," I say, then take a big gulp of cold black syrup so I have something to choke on other than hysterical laughter in the face of our mutually fucked future and my own profoundly idiotic lie. I actually think the words *Poor Ethan.*

Then he says, "If I lose this place they're going to make me go to business school." *They* meaning his family, and in a heartbeat the spore of sympathy I had for him twists itself inside out, grows to a thousand times its original size, becomes a blood-colored hate-mushroom big enough to block out the sky.

"Ethan," I say to him, "we've known each other a long time, and I've always helped you."

"That's true, Brian. You're a true friend. I love you."

"Do you want my help now?"

"More than anything."

"Then put the motor oil down and listen."

Ethan does as I tell him. He reaches into his pocket, comes out with a blue pen, a notepad like the waitresses use, and his bag of coke. He pours the lines while I cut up a drinking straw. We get to work.

HQ scrapes the company name off the glass on the front door and takes all our swag away: the T-shirts and the menus and the secret sauce recipe card and the vinyl banners and the napkins—if their logo's on it it disappears. I couldn't have asked for a more thorough de-shrooming than the one they give us. Ethan keeps the lease on the space itself.

We're closed for a month for the reboot. The sound system goes back to the plantation. The pinball machine follows close behind. Banquettes and bar stools reupholstered in leather. Pearlescent earth tones floor to ceiling, sconces wherever they'll fit. We become "dazzlingly understated nouveau recherché"— that's a quote from the local paper in their five-star review. And granted it's the same schmuck who gave four stars to both Panera and Carrabba's, but his is the voice that matters in this

town, and anyway we snagged that elusive fifth star. It's just us
and Outback on the mountaintop, here in flatland.

Our waitresses—and, holy shit, waiters!—wear black jeans
and crisp black button-ups. We still favor young people, indeed
hire back as many of the Melissa/Jessicas as will get down with the
brave new vibe. Their friends don't come in for lunch anymore—
we're not even open for lunch on weekdays—but sometimes their
teachers turn up. The adjunct profs, that fraud gentry, save up
all semester for a big night out, and we show them their idea of
a classy time. The new menu's littered with the word "artisanal"
instead of the word "organic"—though obviously "organic" is on
there, too. It's mostly the same food as before, only served on ceramic plates the size of manhole covers at triple the price. The day
we put the new sign up, Polina took a picture on her phone and
texted it to her father. The place is called Sungold, duh.

We still haven't managed to find a black person willing to
work with us but it's something we're interested in pursuing.
Is it weird that we talk about it? That we agree? I understand
that they—like women, right?—are not some homogenous body
made up of interchangeable units any one of which might as
well be any other and/or representative of the whole. That's a
pernicious cultural fantasy—words that still stick in my throat
a bit when I use them, but the point is I *do* use them, even have
some sense of what they mean. Anyway we love their music and
think they're cool and wish we knew some. One day one's bound
to walk in here—after all, isn't that what Polina did?

Ethan's still the owner but he keeps his distance. We have
a verbal agreement, a kind of off-the-books restraining order.

I was going to make it a blood oath but didn't want to mix my fluids with his. He's still on thin ice with his family, but Sungold turns a profit so they're provisionally impressed. The ice is thickening: going from something legitimately dangerous to something merely frozen to the core. If they're still waiting for the other shoe to drop, they're going to be waiting a long time because Polina and I manage Sungold as a team and it's a tight operation. No more on-the-clock hummers in the walk-in freezer. No more Captain Morgan going missing by the case. Nobody robs Ethan except for us, and we keep things slow and steady—the goose will lay golden eggs until the day his heart bursts or his liver turns to foie gras. Then I guess I'll have to meet his mom.

One Melissa/Jessica who did not come back to work for us is the one who helped me out of the mushroom suit, the one who showed an interest in my slimed physique, not to mention a rare enthusiasm for putting up with my shit. At Polina's encouragement I called her and asked her to dinner. It was supposed to be chaste, a proper thank-you for having saved me from brain death, but you know how these things go. Her name turns out to be Kaylee Boyd, peach-colored all-American Dave Matthews fan, but beyond that rife with specific attributes and qualities of all kinds. For example, she studies environmental science, is working on a model to predict the rate at which our landlocked town will become beachfront property, then a water park, then a coral reef—though of course, she's quick to qualify, coral will be a history lesson by that point, so something else will take over our drowned houses, or nothing will. That part's harder to guess about. It's all terrifying. I mostly tune it out.

Here's what it comes down to. Kaylee is a woman who looks like a photograph of a woman. A photograph you look at and go, *Oh come on* that's *not real.* And you'd think that because of this, being with her would feel like being in one of those photographs, but it doesn't. It feels . . . different, somehow, not like that at all.

"So what does it feel like?" Polina asks me. It's late. We've sent everyone home and are sitting at the bar, tired after a long night's work but happy, relaxing in sconce light, drinking nightcaps of Ethan's Macallan twelve-year while we finish up ripping him off. I'm not sure how to answer her question.

"Normal, I guess. Or like, I don't know, being alive."

A TALKING CURE

My name is Lacey Anne Schmidt. My fiancé's name—which I still haven't decided whether I'll take or not—is as or more plain. He is Zachary Davis, black-haired and lanky with a little beer belly that pooches over the waist of his slacks. If I take his name I will be Lacey Anne Davis, or Lacey Anne Schmidt-Davis, though I think Davis-Schmidt sounds better, though I'm pretty sure that's not how it's supposed to go. I mean in terms of the order of the names when a woman takes a man's. Meanwhile there remains the problem of my first name. I can never decide if I hate "Lacey" because it's so white trash or so country club, but one way or the other it sounds terribly unserious, and so when I publish it's going to be as Anne Schmidt, or Anne Schmidt-Davis, which I think has a decent cadence to it, like Eve Kosofsky-Sedgwick or Claude Lévi-Strauss.

Forgive me if my references trend obscure. Zachary and I are both PhD candidates at UPenn. I'm New Media and he's Comp Lit, which means, at the risk of totally overdetermining your reading of this story, that the common ground of our respective theoretical apparatuses starts and ends with Freud. Zachary's dissertation is on ideations of Confederate masculinity in late twentieth-century Southern fiction, i.e., post Faulkner and O'Connor. He's writing about Barry Hannah's obsession with J. E. B. Stuart in *Airships*, and Padgett Powell's with Nathan Bedford Forrest in *Mrs. Hollingsworth's Men*. Also "Shiloh" by Bobbie Ann Mason, where the woman leaves the trucker after they visit the hallowed grounds, etc.—though the way things have been going these past few months, it's not clear Zachary's writing anything about anybody. He's been completely blocked.

We live together in a third-floor apartment near campus and are both ABD. We've been dating for about three years, and engaged for exactly seven weeks. It's Friday night. We're getting home—late—from a reception at the school followed by a few nightcaps with some of our fellow grad students. Both of us are drunk, and I've got this idea in my head that we should do our own version of the truth session from "Water Liars," that Barry Hannah story where the husband and the wife tell each other about their sexual pasts.

At first Zachary doesn't want to, but I kind of stick it to him so he says, Okay, sure. So I get another set of nightcaps going and we start. But the thing of it is, even though we're about the same age as the people in the story, that couple had been married for ten years already. What I mean is that they had plenty of—how to put this?—distance from what they were talking about. And of course the point of "Water Liars" is how the wife's news sends the husband for a brutal loop anyway—distance nothing. Distance be damned.

Zachary proposed to me in Locust Grove, Virginia, about four hours down from Philly. We were on a kind of vision quest for his project (the truth session hardly our first experiment with voodoo academia), visiting the grave of Stonewall Jackson's arm at Ellwood Manor—Jackson himself of course lying in Lexington in a cemetery that bears his name.

I'd looked online and found a couple of wineries nearby in Spotsylvania and a place in town to stay. Not exactly two weeks in Paris, or even a long weekend in the Poconos, but it was something: what we could swing.

The funny thing—well, one funny thing—about the grave of Stonewall Jackson's arm is that it is not, technically, a grave anymore, and indeed it may never have been. Nobody's sure. We'd read online that in 1998 the park service dug up the plot to install a piece of concrete to keep looters out, and when they did this they discovered that the legendary metal box containing the arm, the very thing they meant to protect, wasn't there to be protected. But Zachary said this didn't change his desire to see the site. If it was a fraud, he said, that was interesting, too, albeit in a different way.

Forgive me one last digression, but my inner second-wave feminist thinks it's obscene that I've spent this much time discussing my boyfriend's—ahem, fiancé's—work without mentioning my own. And who am I to say she's wrong? So. My work concerns the appropriation of mythological and folk motifs for use in massively multiplayer online role-playing games. I buy high-level characters from burnt-out gamers, and these allow me access to the most remote realms of the virtual worlds without my having to spend thousands of hours building up experience points in a half dozen different games.

Zachary played *Spells of Evermore 3* with me once. I had a barbarian warrior and a wood elf druid, and I needed him to play the druid, backing me up while I fought this one particular dragon. His job was to alternately cast ensnaring vines on the monster and healing spells on me. So basically he had to press two buttons. But the dragon had these minions and one of them was a necromancer and things got out of hand, and I admit I may have overreacted when we both got killed, but that was because I knew it was going to be a fucking week of my life to get the lost experience points back when slaying the dragon hadn't even been the goal in the first place. We were only killing him to get his eyes so we could go see some witch who supposedly had been modeled on Baba Yaga. Zachary said I was no fun to play with and I reminded him that the point of the game wasn't to have fun, and that was the last time I asked him to take an active interest in my work.

But getting back to our truth session. Because it's not 1971 or whatever year it's supposed to be in the Hannah story, we're having a tough time finding stuff that the other person doesn't already know. We know each other's loss-of-virginity episodes and we know each other's numbers. He knows about my abortion. I know he messed around with guys a few times in college. All very healthy and progressive, I'm sure, but the point is that before we know it we've run out of revelations from our pasts and have stumbled into the veritable present.

So I admit that, yes, I sometimes fake with him. Not often, I'm quick to add, trying to be kind here and pulling it off, I think, though this is admittedly something I've been looking for a way to talk about.

"Well, when was the last time?" He isn't looking at me. He's at the counter, fixing us fresh drinks. Gin and tonics with zests of lime, because even though we can joke knowingly about "the peculiar institution" and "the War of Northern Aggression" we are still people who live in Philadelphia with their citrus zester. Anyway, I give him the truthful answer about my faking: "Tuesday."

"I see." His tone is relaxed. Casual introspection. If he's hurt he hides it well. Or, also plausible, I'm too drunk to read him.

"Your turn," I say. It occurs to me that we're doing our truth session backwards. In the story they have this great night out— it's the guy's birthday—and then they get into it the morning after, when they're sober, after ditching a party and reaffirming their love. But it's too late to offer this observation, with him already in the middle of talking about Bridget, the girl he dated before me. How it only lasted a few months but was super heavy while it did. I already know all this, I want to say to him. Well, here's some news. Bridget used to be into some rough stuff—she liked to be choked and held down, tossed around. Your average rape fantasy, it sounds like. And he's got his hands in the air, palms out, preemptive defense, saying how he didn't even want to do it at first—refused to role-play the oppressor, was worried he might injure her, etc. But then he learned that simulating violence in a safe space can be a valid way of gaining psychological mastery over trauma. (One wonders what ol' Bridget's truth session might have sounded like.) Long story short, he came around.

I'm wondering, Is this a real story, or is it more like his own roundabout way of asking for— Oh, but I shouldn't be stupid. Besides, if he wants it, he's going to have to say so, or else make a move. Not that I'm in a huge hurry to be gagged with my own underwear, but being pinned at the wrists and bent over the coffee table might make for a nice change of pace. What I won't stand for, however, is this "I'm sending you a signal to make me the offer" shit. Of course, he's gotten pretty good about asking for what he wants—which, by the way, I credit myself with having taught him because I remember what it was like when we first got together—so maybe this is just the drunken truth slopping out. Speaking of which.

"I gave Evan Stanz a blow job," I say. Evan is Zachary's best friend. They grew up together, and both did their undergrad at Wesleyan. Now Evan lives in Chicago. He works in real estate and on the weekends plays bass in a grunge nostalgia band. The first time Evan visited after we had started dating, he slept on Zachary's couch for four nights. We'd been together about three months at the time.

My fingers are drumming on the table. Zachary drains his drink. Would you believe that I did not engineer this whole conversation to lead up to betraying myself in this way? At least not consciously. But it's worth stressing that even in retrospect my confession does not feel inevitable—it has taken us both by surprise.

"That night was the first time I was ever really, like *really* mad at you," I say, exponentially more amazed with myself every moment that words keep coming out of my mouth. "You remember how we fought? And I was thinking I was going to break up with you, that's how mad I was, and—oh, fuck it, I wanted to."

"Were you trying to get caught?"

"God, no. I waited until you were asleep. Evan was asleep, too. I had to wake him. I told him to be quiet, and that if he ever breathed a word of it I'd deny the whole thing. We didn't fuck. He didn't touch me at all. I did what I wanted to do, and then it was over."

"Did you swallow?" he asks, trying to do the ice-cold thing, though to sell it he'd have to be able to look me in the eye.

"You're taking this rather in stride," I say. "And also, fuck you."

"Just tell me if you did."

"You're being disgusting."

"I'm curious."

"Well, I wasn't going to spit it on the floor, was I?"

"Lacey Anne," he says, and it's like, Okay, so we're done being hard-asses now.

"If I had it back, I mean if I could do that night over—"

"He told me."

"Excuse me?"

"He told me."

"Told you."

"When I told him I was going to propose. He said he couldn't live with himself if he didn't."

I feel the bottom drop out of my stomach. Here I've been keeping this terrible secret close, nursing it with my guilt. And then it turns out that the boys have long since settled the matter among themselves. How nice for them.

"Well, did he think I was good?" I ask.

He ignores my question. We bask in our silence, maybe zone in on the green of the microwave display clock—if you squint hard you can make the LED quiver, the numbers swimming apart into fragments before your blurring vision, your watering eyes. I can hear cars idling at the light. Someone's blasting dance music.

Then he breaks the silence, says, "You want to know something funny?"

"Something funny? Oh, yeah. I mean, you bet."

"Maybe 'funny' isn't the word. I don't know, I never expected to say this, but since we're talking I guess I might as well tell you that when you told me the thing about you and Evan— well, I mean when he told me the thing, but then, seriously, again when you said it just before—both times the first feeling I had wasn't anger or hurt. I swear to God, Lacey Anne, it was straight-up jealousy. I was in love with him for a long time. The whole time we were growing up, I guess. I'd have done anything for him, I really would have, or with him, not that I ever tried, or I mean there was never any question of—but it's like, if just once, you know, like if I could have ever put it out there and had to own it, maybe my whole life would have been different. I don't know. And not that there's anything wrong with my life now, but—well, it made me feel bad for that past version of myself, that's all. That kid. He ached so fucking much."

"Baby," I say, meaning it.

He stands up and so I do, too, though I'm not sure where we're supposed to be going. It's as if I'm watching myself—watching us—from somewhere else, not like the God's eye view from the ceiling but maybe like a pervert on the fire escape, peeping in. As Zachary rounds the table I grab my dress by the skirt and in one fluid but graceless motion pull it over my head and off my body. I ball it up and chuck it at him. He catches it and throws it down. We end up on the couch, tangled, neither one of us speaking but both of us thinking the same thing: Is this the spot where it happened? Is this?

There are several competing theories about where Stonewall's arm might be. Marauding Union men is the popular one, though considered unlikely by serious historians. It may have been stolen in the 1920s; there's a whole school of thought about that. The notion I find most compelling postulates that the original marker was never meant to designate the exact burial plot but rather the field of battle where the injury was sustained. Everything else, says this theory, has been one long misunderstanding.

At the winery we took the tour and then spent some time tasting. There was a Cabernet with a blackberry thing happening that I liked. We bought three bottles and asked the sommelier if he knew of a decent place in town to eat. Zachary would propose to me the next day beneath an oak on a green slope at noon, and I would of course say yes, and we would kiss and start ourselves, our lives, careening toward everything that I've already shared. But let's stick for a minute with the night before the proposal. In our suite at the Red Roof Inn there was a little coffee maker by the sink. I took the two plastic cups out of their plastic packaging while Zachary opened one of our bottles. We shut off the overhead light, then turned on both bedside lamps and the shower. We left the bathroom door open and the bathroom light off. The water was warm, then all of a sudden too hot. I wanted to get it perfect. A little steam's okay, but nothing scalding. We climbed in. Zachary worked the soap between my legs, exploring me as if for the first time, as if he didn't already know me by heart. I reached back. He said, "Lacey Anne." He loves to breathe my name when he's inside me, and it is the only time that I genuinely enjoy hearing it said, because it's like everything I love and hate about myself somehow comes together, and I feel exposed and completed, named and found.

Which is a good line to end on, though it must be obvious by this point that neither of us is the type to leave well enough alone, so I may as well tell what happens next.

He picks the boy out—a student from the 201 class he taught last semester. He says there were hints dropped, inklings. They've kept in touch.

The boy, Blake, comes on a Wednesday. He knocks on our door even though we cracked it open for him when we buzzed him into the building. Zachary is sitting on the couch, watching something on TV he doesn't care about. A sport. I'm checking the spaghetti sauce. It's sauce, all right. "Nearly done," I say as I turn toward the knocking, which has nudged the door fully open. He stands in the doorway, obviously nervous but trying hard not to show that he is. I do not try to hide that I'm sizing him up. He ought to know it. He's taller than either of us, and somewhat bedraggled-looking in dirty white jeans and a pair of beat-up Converse All Stars. He wears a thin yellow T-shirt with a mud-colored corporate logo, a red bandana tied loose about his neck. His beard is patchy. He's holding a six-pack of PBR in a plastic bodega bag with a black-eyed smiley face above the blue words THANK YOU THANK YOU THANK YOU. The smiley face is the same color as his T-shirt must have been when it was new.

"Hi," I say to Blake as I approach him. I open my arms and we briefly embrace. He smells clean and fresh, not like cigarettes. For some reason I'd thought of him as a smoker, which maybe is my way of saying, Kids these days. Zachary hustles over to join us, but I let the boy slip from my arms to his. A sort of handoff. I'm back at the stove. Let them have this moment, if they can wring a moment out of whatever is happening. I keep my back turned, one hand holding the wooden sauce spoon, stirring.

The boys sit. I serve dinner. We drink ourselves comfortable. Together we move to the increasingly storied couch, undressing one another, but Blake can't seem to get in the mood.

Finally, he reaches down and eases Zachary's head from between his pale legs, his flaccid penis shiny like a slug. "Hey, it's okay," he says to Zachary, as though he were the wiser of the two of them, the three of us. "Let me do you," he says, but then instead of switching places with Zachary scoots over to the far end of the couch and draws his legs up under himself like a nesting animal. I reach out and take Zachary's hand, pull him over to me. Blake watches us as though we were a reasonably compelling foreign film. He waits until we finish, then gets dressed and says good night.

"It's better like this," Zachary says when we're alone again.

"I think you're right," I say and take him into my arms. As we rock slowly back and forth, heads on shoulders, I notice our reflection in the dark glass face of the TV. We look like we're bobbing in a rowboat, on a lake or out to sea. It occurs to me to wonder: *Is this what a marriage is?* And then a related question: *So what if it's not?*

ADON OLAM

Over the sixth grade holiday break—1993, this would have been, heading into '94—my friend Isaac Adelman began to suspect that something was off about his twin brother, Jake. They were identical, but lately Jake had been getting short of breath when we played half-court in their front driveway, and when we went swimming—nothing special in South Florida in December—Jake wouldn't race with us or have a diving contest or anything. "I'll be judge," he said, glum and defensive as he climbed onto the green raft and gave himself a push toward the shallow end of the pool.

So Isaac and I saw who of the two of us could jump farther (me), and who could hold his breath the longest (me), and who could do the fastest lap, which was such a close call that we really did need Jake to judge for us, but Jake had fallen asleep. He was lying on his side on the raft, half curled up, with his eyes closed and mouth open, one arm across his face to block the sunlight, the other arm dangling in the water.

The pediatrician took X-rays. A sarcoma was putting pressure on Jake's left lung as well as his heart. Everything changed in the Adelman house after that. For example, the twins had always shared one huge room upstairs, but now Jake was to be moved to the first floor, down the hall from his parents and next door to Claudette, the housekeeper, in what had been Mr. Adelman's home office. To offset the sickroom atmosphere, Mr. and Mrs. Adelman splurged on electronics and toys. They got a three-disc CD changer with speakers, a new TV and VCR for each of their rooms, and every game system you could think of—Super Nintendo, Neo Geo, Sega CD, Game Boys for the long hours in doctors' waiting rooms. They had lava lamps and Nerf guns and remote-controlled cars.

My mother encouraged me to spend time with the twins. They needed me, she said, to bring some cheer into the house and to offer my "moral support." She said I made things feel more normal over there. And of course we would have offered to reciprocate, but Jake couldn't go on sleepovers, and she wouldn't want the poor sick boy to feel left out if just Isaac came over, besides which she imagined that Mrs. Adelman must not want to split the boys up more than they already were, what with their room situation and Jake's having been pulled out of school.

When I slept over we were allowed to stay up as late as we wanted playing video games and watching movies. If Jake had an appetite it was like a miracle. They'd have Claudette make anything he asked for. And there was always stuff to snack on—Fruit Roll-Ups and Kudos bars, fresh-made peanut butter oatmeal cookies and frozen yogurt. They had this big ceramic bowl—Mrs. Adelman had made it in a class she took—that sat on the breakfast bar and was always filled with clementine oranges. I would beg my mom to buy us some when she went to the store.

Mr. and Mrs. Adelman were usually in bed by ten thirty, and it was never long after that before Claudette retired to her room to watch TV with her headphones on. By this point Jake would have fallen asleep during whatever movie we'd chosen after dinner. I'd nudge him awake and help him down to his room while Isaac set the timer on his digital stopwatch for fifteen minutes. We'd pass the time playing *Street Fighter II Turbo*. He always had to be Ryu, who wore a white karate suit and had a hurricane kick and shot energy blasts out of his hands. I liked Guile, the American special ops vet with camo pants and a flat top, but I could kick Isaac's ass so fast with Guile that it wasn't fun for either of us, so I'd usually hit random and let the computer decide, though if it made me be Chun-Li—the Chinese girl—then we had to reset. When the stopwatch beeped we'd peek down from the top of the stairs for one last security check, then shut Isaac's bedroom door.

When Mr. Adelman converted his office into a room for Jake, he'd moved some boxes into the front hall closet underneath the stairs. While most contained tax returns and business records, one had turned out to be full of dirty magazines. Isaac had grabbed a handful of these and stashed them in his closet, in the boxes of board games and the deep pockets of winter coats.

Isaac alone got to choose which magazine we looked at and the pace at which the glossy pages turned. He liked to talk about the girls in the pictures, what they were doing and the guys they were doing it with and if we'd ever be like them. We compared which of us had a bigger thing, and more hair around it, and who could shoot more stuff, which was pretty much impossible to determine as long as we were shooting into socks from the laundry since the point of the sock was to absorb the stuff, so we stopped using them and did it into each other's hands instead but it was still hard to tell. He tried to make it seem like these were just more games we were playing, friendly competitions like pool jumps or *Street Fighter* rounds or whatever. When Jake got better, Isaac said, we could all play.

I wanted to tell him to shut up about it, but I didn't know how. (Plus I knew if I made him angry he might take the magazine away.) I wished that he had gotten sick instead of his brother, who was bald now, thinner every time I saw him, and wheezing in his sleep so bad that when the house settled at night you could hear it from all the way upstairs.

Jake's funeral was the first one I ever went to. It was an overcast April morning, and I remember how the family lined up to receive the mourners: his mom's mascara running, Isaac flanked by his grandparents and pallid in a suit he'd half outgrown, eyes glued to his shoes. And Mr. Adelman, how impossibly tall he seemed, leaning down and in close to shake my hand. I remember his big wet eyes and how I avoided them, terrified his grief might somehow allow him to read my secrets if I met his gaze. I don't remember the service, only afterward, standing by the open grave, and even that I don't think I remember the way it happened. There must have been a crowd gathered, a rabbi, my mother's hand on my shoulder, but my mind seems to have erased all these things, or else never recorded them in the first place. I can see the green mat they put out, smell the fresh earth, feel the humidity of the day—all of it eerily clear in my mind—but I can also see myself alone beside the gravestone, which makes no sense, because as Jews we don't unveil the stone until a year after the burial—there's this whole other ceremony for it—besides which, if it had really been the way I remember, wouldn't the memory be of the view looking out through my own eyes instead of a picture of myself standing there?

Isaac had a new suit, a blue one that fit him, for our sixth grade graduation, which was held in the library, a spacious open-plan building with a tall peaked roof. They pushed all the rolling shelves against the walls and brought a makeshift stage in and folding chairs for the parents. Our principal gave a speech, and so did Dr. Joshua Mizzum, a local orthodontist who was running for school board. After that the chorus sang "Don't Stop Thinking About Tomorrow" and then the principal came back up to read all of our names. They included Jake's with the rest of the class, and he got a standing ovation. Boys in pulled-loose ties clapped and cheered while girls who had never spoken a word to either twin dabbed away fat jewel-like tears.

The Adelmans went away that summer, and the next year Isaac's parents enrolled him in a private school. He took a bus and wore a uniform and had all new friends. My mother never pressed me about it. I think that as far as she was concerned I had done my job.

This was a lonely time for me. Our house was on a lake and there was this one part, down our block a ways, where the road went over a canal. I liked to spend time there. I'd hop a low fence, scuttle down eight or maybe ten feet of embankment, not too steep. A skinny oak stood at the shoreline, leaning out over the smooth, still water so a mirror tree hung in the lake, its limbs like arms reaching down into a dull sky at the bottom of the world. Instead of going to the tree, you turned around and then could duck into the culvert. It had a concrete ledge big enough to sit comfortably on. The cars going by on the road above made a low pervasive thrum, and if you raised your voice you got killer echo. As near as I could tell nobody else knew about it. I'd go down there with comic books, or a box of matches and a few of my old G.I. Joes, even my homework if I was bored enough.

Sometimes I would sing down there, songs by bands I liked or older stuff off records my mom played or even songs they'd made us learn in Hebrew school—anything I knew by heart. I sang "Adon Olam," which was my favorite Jewish song, mostly because of its melody, which was like, I don't know, swaying or something, but also it had these, like, zigzags in it. I mean it felt powerful somehow, significant, almost haunted—if you can be haunted in a good way. I liked to sing as loudly as I could and go slow, stretch each line out so the echoes piled up on each other and I would keep my eyes shut tight and feel like I was disappearing into the noise, or else becoming it. Vortex, I thought.

Wormhole. Black hole. Vacuum. B'terem kol. In English this meant "before the creation," or "before form." What the song was saying was that God is God of everything even when there's nothing to be God of. Which was exactly how I felt when I was down there: a God of nothing.

For my sixteenth birthday my mom gave me her '91 Buick Skylark, free and clear, having leased herself a certified preowned Volvo. But she warned me that she was only paying for gas until the end of the school year, which meant I was going to need a summer job. Which is how Isaac Adelman came back into my life again, in the summer of 1998, at a day camp run out of the local JCC, where we'd both applied to be junior counselors and had been assigned to work together.

Our senior counselor was three years older, a college girl home for the summer. Alana Shekhin had gone to my high school but had been a senior when I was a freshman. I knew she'd been in Honor Society and run with the J.A.P. crowd, into which she'd blended well enough to have never figured in any but my most depraved locker room fantasies. But the year away had been good to her. She'd let her hair grow past her shoulders and had a silver nose stud that the camp wouldn't let her wear while she was on duty. I would see her at the end of the day, sitting in her car, putting it back in before she turned the ignition. She had a flat stomach but a thick waist, strong legs topped by a world-class fat Jewish ass crammed into a small pair of khaki shorts. She wore a gold chai charm on a thin gold chain.

Isaac wore a gold chain, too, but a thicker one, with no charm. He had a fade in his hair, baggy basketball shorts low on his hips, and spotless white Nike Airs. I wore whatever. Brown or beige cargoes, a pair of scuffed Vans or my old black Airwalks with the little carrot insignia stitched on the tongue. I'd had them since eighth grade and considered them my lucky sneakers, despite being vaguely ashamed that they still fit, though I told myself they would have been unbearably tight if they hadn't been so worn in.

And all of us in our requisite camp T-shirts, pale-yellow fabric with blue text and graphics: an anthropomorphic Star of David grinned and made jazz hands below a clip-art banner that read, CAMP KLIPPOT KETANOT 5758 / 1998!!!!

Our campers were six years old, or would be soon. Isaac's mission seemed to be to avoid interacting with them at all costs. He didn't craft; he didn't help with bathroom runs or changing the kids for swim. Alana took the ten girls and I took the eight boys and we split for our separate locker rooms while Isaac stood poolside, checking his pager. Alana and I made up splashing games for the kids to play, encouraged them to dunk their heads underwater, kept them amused and alive.

We had this one girl, Brianne, small for her age and skittish, who always brought goggles to the pool because she was terrified of the sting of chlorine. When they slipped off her head she flailed in place, crying out for help. I carried her to the edge and told her to hang onto the wall. I retrieved the goggles but didn't give them back right away. I expanded the strap as far as it would go and slipped them on. They were

Disney Princess goggles and I could barely get them around my head—but managed to, finally, and sank down below the surface and beheld the white, strong, scissoring, large-pored legs of Alana Shekhin, who wore a modest dark-blue one-piece, but the Lycra couldn't help but bulge and cleft. She was in the deep end with some of the more confident swimmers and I was in heaven. Then the elastic on the goggles snapped and my eyes were flooded with chlorine. The kid had been right: maintenance nuked this pool. I surfaced, eyes burning, and made my way back to Brianne.

"Honey," I said, "I've got some bad news."

I was rarely in a hurry to get home when camp let out, so most days I stuck around at the JCC and used the gym. Once or twice a week I'd follow Isaac in his F-150 over to the park, where he'd sell me a half-eighth for twenty-five bucks and we'd match bowls and talk shit about Camp Klippot. We made jokes about our campers—the pisser, the crier, the clinger, and Benjamin Schneer, this freaky kid in our group who hardly talked or blinked and devoted every art class to drawing elaborate mazes that he then gave to the other kids to try and solve.

I had to hand it to Isaac—he did great impressions of the kids. I admired that. I didn't know how to be anybody but myself, and half the time it felt like I wasn't even pulling that off. But in the park it was all okay. We smoked and laughed and bullshitted, secure in the knowledge that our jobs were pointless, all the rules we had to follow were stupid, and every last one of our wards was a head case, doomed to fail at life.

"Well, there's Alana at least," I said. "In that bathing suit."

"Fuck that," Isaac said. "Fuck that bitch and her fucking attitude." He was mad because she'd banned him from picking up the kids' afternoon snack from the commissary. This was a job he loved doing—the only job he loved doing, indeed the only job he did—because it meant he could swing by the pay phone in the lobby and call back whoever had beeped him since lunch; plus it meant he got to choose the snack. Isaac picked Nutty Bars every time. Nutty Bars were kind of like giant Kit Kat bars crossed with some Reese's knockoff you'd find at Dollar Tree. Alana hated Nutty Bars. She described them, with uncharacteristic candor, as packing foam filled with imitation peanut butter and slathered in genuine dog shit. Isaac refused to take Alana's preference into account, so she had decreed that picking up afternoon snack was my job now. Personally, I didn't care what the snack was because I didn't eat it. I brought clementines from home and ate those. Which reminded me—I still had one left! I took it out of my pocket and stuck my thumb into the rind and unraveled it in a long thin spiral, unbroken, while Isaac loaded us up a new bowl with weed from the bag he'd just sold me. We sat there passing the bowl back and forth, the only sounds the flick of the lighter, the low whistle of the carb, and the buzz of the woods: dragonflies, birds, and mosquitoes; squirrels scrambling through the carpet of fallen leaves. We never once talked about his brother, or the fact that we had used to be friends.

The next day was a Friday and Isaac was absent from camp. I couldn't believe how much better the day went. Alana and I made a good team—no, a great one. I did whatever she asked me to and made her laugh. When I picked up the snack I got her favorite: those chocolate cupcakes with white frosting in the center and the curlicue of icing across the top.

Benjamin Schneer came up to me holding a big piece of green construction paper covered in close-set curving purple lines, like something halfway between Arab calligraphy and a pile of intestines. It was one of his mazes. He held the paper flat on the palm of one hand like a tiny waiter; in his other hand was a yellow crayon for me to use. "I forgot to make an exit on this one," he said solemnly, "but you can still try." So I sat there and worked my way through his sealed maze while he watched me, making all the wrong turns and hitting all the dead ends until every purple pathway was filled with a yellow line. I put the crayon down. He took the paper back and walked away without saying another word.

Before we knew it Alana and I had strapped our last kid into her car seat and were walking together through the parking lot. I asked her if she wanted to get high and her eyes lit up. She asked if there was somewhere we could go. I told her there was and she said she'd follow me.

I didn't want to go to the park in case Isaac was there, so I decided to bring Alana to my spot under the road. I had never shown it to anyone before and felt like this made our outing into a kind of adventure. We parked our cars at my house and walked down the block. I went down the embankment first, offering my hand to her to help her down, and we continued to hold hands as I showed her the skinny oak that made the mirror tree, then led her around the corner and onto the concrete ledge. We sat with our legs hanging out over the water and our backs against the curved stone wall, which felt cool through my shirt even though it was a hot day. Naturally, I gave her greens.

"Oh, wow," she said, coughing out a thick cloud of smoke. "This shit is great. I thought you were never going to ask me."

"Well, I sometimes smoke with Isaac," I said. "And he can be pretty weird about stuff."

"You know what? Fuck that dipshit pain-in-the-ass. I don't care if he is my cousin." She passed the bowl to me. I hit it and passed it back.

"Wait, hang on—Isaac's your cousin?"

"Yeah. That's why he's in my group. My aunt wants me to help straighten him out or keep an eye on him or something, and she's on the J's board, so even though he's like a walking child neglect lawsuit they have to put up with him." She passed the bowl back. The cherry was burning. "Did you know he had a twin brother?"

"Seriously? Isaac's a twin?" I took my hit while she answered so I didn't have to worry about the look on my face. I made a little show of holding the smoke in and blowing it out through my nose while I listened to her.

"They were identical. Like, they'd switch places at dinner and you wouldn't know it. His brother's name was Jake. He had cancer."

"Oh, shit. I'm so sorry."

"It's okay. I mean it was awful, but it was, I don't know, like four years ago now. Anyway Isaac's mom is convinced that that's what his problems are all about. His gangsta bullshit and every-thing. She donated like half a building to his high school to keep them from kicking him out this year. God knows what she gives to the J. And he freaks out every time she suggests therapy, so here we all are. I just hope he's not ruining your whole summer, too. Jesus, wow, sorry to lay all that on you. So TMI, I'm sure."

"Oh, no way," I said. "I'm glad that you told me. Things make a lot more sense now." We sat there with our backs to the wall and the cashed bowl cooling between us. I asked her if she wanted to share a clementine. She said sure and watched my fingers as I worked the rind.

I tossed the spiral peel into the green-brown water. We watched it splash down and resurface, then float off. Leaves and bits of trash bobbed by as well. I halved the fruit and held her piece out to her and our fingers brushed when she took it. She ate hers section by section. I put my whole share in my mouth and chewed it up. I wiped my hands on my shorts and then put the bowl away. Now there was only empty space between us. Alana shifted position, stretched her legs out on the concrete, leaned back and let her head rest in my lap. I knew she could feel me through my zipper, poking at the back of her skull. "Listen," she said, "I've got a boyfriend at school so we can't go all the way. That's like my serious rule."

"Okay," I said. "Yeah, that works, sure. We can just do whatever you want."

"You're a good guy, Adam," she said. "Do you know that?"
I told her I did.

• • •

Isaac was back at camp on Monday, no explanation offered (or sought) for his absence, and Alana went back into senior counselor mode—bubbly and solicitous with the kids, curt and impersonal with the two of us. Did she regret what had happened, or was she being overly cautious about her cousin finding out? Maybe, I thought, she was as sorry to see him again as I was.

When snack time came around that afternoon, Isaac walked out of our room without a word. He returned fifteen minutes later, red-eyed and reeking, a smirk on his face, the box of Nutty Bars already open. I could feel Alana's rage coming off of her in waves. When he offered her a Nutty Bar she smacked it out of his hand. It spun across the floor and a couple of our campers gasped. "Hey," I said to her. "Do you want a clementine?" Ignoring my question, she walked over to her cubby, dug around in her purse for a granola bar, and took it outside to eat alone. Isaac shrugged, picked Alana's Nutty Bar up off the floor, unwrapped it, and took a big bite. "Bitch," he said.

"Ooooh," said Brianne. "You said a swear."

"True. But that's gonna stay our little secret because otherwise you might never get snack again ever, which wouldn't be too fun—right?" Brianne nodded, her eyes already wet. He surveyed the crowd of small faces looking up at us. "That goes for all you bitches," he said.

That night I dreamed that I was swimming at the Adelmans' like old times but Alana was there, too, only she was her real age but me and Isaac were young again. Jake wasn't around. It was dark out and the pool light was bright as the moon—a moon at the bottom of the pool. I saw Isaac standing on the top step at the shallow end. "Let's see who—" I said, but didn't finish because I heard that my voice wasn't mine; it was Jake's voice, and I realized then that I was Jake, or part of me was, that when he had died a spark of his soul had joined with mine so I carried him with me, and so did Isaac, and so we had these strange sparks in us that could never be absorbed or expelled. Alana dove deep into the water, all the way to the bottom of the pool where she swam in tight circles, going faster, a dark form outlined in churning brightness, which was the last thing I saw before I woke up with a seizing pressure in my lungs like I'd stayed underwater too long or slept with a stone on my chest.

It was a quarter to six, dishwater light trickling through my blinds, and I could have gone back to sleep for another half hour, maybe forty-five minutes if I'd wanted to. But I didn't want to. I didn't want to go back to that other world for anything. Instead I closed my eyes and slipped my hand into my boxers and thought about Alana and the things we'd done under the road. I thought about the way she'd smelled—lavender soap and pennies—and the sweat under her tits and the impatience with which she'd guided my hand into the slick hot hair between her legs. True to her word, we hadn't gone all the way, but she let me touch her and also did things to me nobody had ever done before, except for Isaac, which the more I thought about it somehow seemed like it shouldn't count, though I knew that it did. And what would Alana say if she ever found out that I'd used to be friends with him, that I'd feigned ignorance about Jake's existence and death? Was Alana the reason he was in our group, as she thought, or had the pairing been about both of us—or just me? Mrs. Adelman wanting to rekindle an old friendship—a "positive influence" is probably how she would have phrased it—or maybe it had somehow been Isaac's idea? And what about me? I wasn't . . . whatever, obviously, because I'd hooked up with Alana and only in general ever usually thought about girls, but then what about what Isaac and I had done? I had hardly thought about him and what we used to do since it had happened, but now all that buried stuff was coming unearthed.

I reached around for something to wipe up with, then decided to get into the shower. It was full light outside and time to start my day.

"Hey, bro," Isaac said. "Don't you think that braces are bullshit? Like they're this giant scam Doc Mizzum's running on us?"

We were at a picnic table in a thickish copse of oak, our usual spot, well off the main path and away from the road. We were sitting on the table with our feet on the bench. My teeth had come in straight—straight enough, my mom had said—so I had never had braces, and therefore hadn't given them much thought other than to count them as one more thing that everyone else but me had in common with each other.

"When do they come off?" I asked.

"He says the end of the year, maybe."

"Nice," I said. "You can ride that out."

"Yeah, unless it's a fucking lie."

We were quiet a minute. I took a deep breath. "Hey," I said. "Have you ever, like, come when you're high?"

"Huh?"

"Like if you're smoking with a girl and she wants to . . . you know, or if you're even stoned by yourself at home and you just decide to go for it."

"Dude, I don't know, why are we even talking about this?"

"I'm just saying if you never tried it, it's, like, pretty cool. Different, you know?"

"I mean high's high," Isaac said. "Everything's better. So what?"

"Hey," I said, easing myself off the table and standing in the dirt before him. "Put the bowl down for a second."

"What the hell, bro," he said—but it wasn't a question. He did as I asked. He put the pipe down on the table next to him, put his hands on his knees, and stared at me, waiting to see what I was going to do. I wondered what he thought I was thinking about, would have given anything to know what he saw when he looked at me. I hit him square in the center of the face with my fist and knew as soon as I made contact that I'd broken his nose, and the skin on my own knuckles. I swung again. He reeled backwards, landed flat on his back, then rolled over onto his side, half curled up, one arm protecting his face and head, the other dangling limp over the edge of the table. There was blood seeping into the wood and dripping between the slats, clotting the dirt below. I climbed onto the tabletop and stood over him and kicked him in the gut. He moaned. Blood ran into his open mouth and I could hear him swallowing it. A crimson bubble appeared between his lips, grew large and thin like chewing gum right before it pops. I wanted him to piss himself but as near as I could tell he hadn't.

I took everything he had, even his pager. As I clipped it to the waistband of my shorts I reminded myself that he was the one who should have gotten sick. He shouldn't have been alive to suffer this. I thought of Mr. and Mrs. Adelman: one son dead and the other this poseur delinquent, this waste. I tried to imagine the chasm between the life they'd planned and the one they were actually living.

"Why are you crying?" Isaac asked me. I could hear in his voice what it was costing him to get each word out. I kicked him in the stomach again. And then I ran away.

Isaac didn't come back to camp, but he didn't rat me out either. After all, what could he have possibly said that wouldn't have gotten him into trouble, too? According to Alana, who heard it through the family, he said he'd been jumped by some punk rock kids.

We were down in the culvert under the road again, for what was probably the last time. Camp was ending. Her boyfriend was coming to visit. He'd be there a week; then they were driving back up to school together. She had her shirt off but her bra on and wanted to know if I could hook her up with some pot. "I know it's a kind of fucked-up thing to ask, but it would make him super happy if we had some and you're like the only person I know with a steady connect. I'll pay you for it, obviously."

"I don't want your money," I said. It was almost true. I gave her the last of what I'd taken from Isaac—sixty, maybe seventy bucks' worth.

"Wow, holy shit, thanks." She opened her purse and tucked the baggie away somewhere inside, then zipped it shut. She took her bra off, folded it, laid it on top of the purse. "God," she said. "What a funny summer this turned out to be."

The summer ended. I started buying my pot from Kenny Beckstein, a hippie kid who could also get mushrooms and LSD. I figured out that half a green gel tab was the perfect dose: you could count on an interesting day but also on being basically sober enough to drive home when the last bell rang. For winter vacation, I bought five tabs to last me two weeks. But then I woke up on Christmas morning with this idea in my head that I should take the remaining three all at once. For Jews Christmas is like this total blank day: no school and parents don't have work, and you can't go out because everything is closed except the movies and the movies are mobbed.

I loaded my pockets with clementines and grabbed my Discman, thinking I'd take a walk around the neighborhood. I thought about going to my spot under the road, but whenever I went there now I thought about Alana, who was away at school, or maybe home for winter break—she never responded to my IMs anymore so I didn't know what was up with her—and I didn't want to think about all that, so instead I turned the Discman volume up as far as it would go and walked right past the embankment on the street that was my old spot's roof, my shitty headphones shrieking, the noise like green fire burning my mind clean, my heart beating in time with the propulsive drumming or maybe my own feet on the pavement; I was running and the clementines bonked against my knees through my cargo pockets and I hoped they wouldn't burst and the Discman was skipping and I couldn't find a good way to hold it where it wouldn't skip but I couldn't stop running, sensed the ground falling away behind me, and then the headphone cord slipped out of the jack and there was this rushing silence like a tidal wave and the loose cord was flying around and whipping me as I wove through the neighborhood, throwing the Discman down and not hearing it shatter—it had either landed in grass or fallen into the nothingness—but I didn't—couldn't—look back to see, focused on getting the headphones off, dropped them, too, and kept running until I came to the elementary school, where I shimmied up a drain pipe and swung myself over an eave onto the lowest point of the peaked roof of the library, where I lay flat on my back and felt sick in my stomach and tried to catch my breath.

The whole sky was alive with pale phantoms, metamorphic clouds like wax bubbles in lava lamps. When I had my breath again I crawled to the top on my hands and knees and belly. It was a fairly easy grade, no worse than the embankment had been, but I had to go slowly, because my knees and fingers wanted to pay attention to every subtle contour in the tiles; my mind flooded with a trillion fragments of worthless glittering information, every stray kernel of grit lit up my skin.

I reached the apex. It was the view that, as children, we'd always imagined having. I could see all the school's outbuildings, its PE field and basketball courts, and big chunks of our neighborhood—the new overpass by the road to the mall. I thought I glimpsed the lake my house was on, but then realized that I wasn't looking in the direction my house was in, so it must have been some other lake, or else only in my head.

Isaac was on the basketball court shooting foul shots by himself, and I felt as if I'd known he was there since I got to the school, that perhaps it was even why I had come. What I mean is that this was one of those times when learning something felt like remembering it. He would stand at the line, dribble, shoot, sink it, chase the ball down, then make his way back to the line, doing dodges and head fakes and spin moves as though outmatching an invisible defender. The basketball was a comet and when he moved his body became one, too. If he looked up, I wondered, would he see me? The angle was against him, and I had the sun at my back.

I watched him and ate the clementines. Peels piled up on the roof all around me, their white innards shining even brighter than their glowing skins. A wind rose and the peels rolled down the roof faces, falling away into the void below, an endless empty darkness that had followed me, yawning open where the ground had been. Shocked by the sight, I scrambled toward the relative safety of the middle of the roof and watched the color drain out of the trees. Everything was coming undone. Isaac had the basketball court and I had the library roof and we were shipwreck survivors on bobbing planks, stuck where we were until whatever had begun was finished and the process reversed itself. What had been unwritten would be

rewritten, the shattered world made whole again. Wouldn't it?
I told myself it must be and wanted to tell Isaac—who, I realized, had no idea that any of this was happening—but he was
too far away to hear me no matter how loudly I cried out to
him, no matter what I might have meant to say.

AFTER ELLEN

Ellen is at her internship with the film festival and Scott is in their gravel driveway, loading his half of everything they own into the Jetta. The small stones crunching beneath his sneakers are the same color as the three o'clock sky. He's composing the Dear John in his head while he packs the car, but he can't seem to get it right—not that it can be got right, ditching her like this, but shouldn't there be a way to make it less bad? He carries crates of records, a Camel Light between his lips, sweat streaking down his naked scalp. The Jetta is midnight blue and his own, though he and Ellen share it; usually he drops her off in the morning, then picks her up around four thirty, five. Today, she's going to take the bus home, ostensibly so that Scott can drive out to the Costco by the airport.

Why is he leaving? Tough to say. From the moment they decided to move to Portland together, he'd known that this evil seed was planted in his heart. He could have, maybe should have, said no when she asked him to come with her, but they'd graduated; there was no reason to stick around their college town in Ohio, and he certainly wasn't going back to Long Island, so—the Great Northwest. Why not? Perhaps he had believed that the feeling would pass. The seed would fail to blossom or the fruit would wither on the vine. Last night they had this talk about adopting a dog—curled up on the couch, they weighed the relative merits of mutts versus purebreds—and suddenly he could see their life together, all mapped out: the proposal and the wedding and the grades the kids would be in when the dog died of old age. Now here he is, twelve hours later, gut-sick and elated, sweaty and sore-armed, all his clothes in duffels and Hefty bags.

It's not too late to call this off. He can unload the car, get a bottle of Côtes du Rhône uncorked and into the decanter. He can get everything back in its right place if he's quick. He can come up with a reason that he never made it to Costco. He can put a knife through the front left tire of his car. He can kiss Ellen when she walks through the door.

He shoves a last duffel in on top of his vinyl, then struggles the trunk shut. What else does he even own? His turntables and headphones, his laptop, its power cord and the cord for his cell phone, a few pairs of shoes. That stuff can all go in the backseat. He'll throw a winter coat over the DJ gear so that it won't get stolen in some rest-stop parking lot. The plan is to drive to his sister Priscilla's place in LA. The trip will take two days if he pushes himself, three if he goes easy. Priscilla, who is four years older, is married to an entertainment lawyer. They have a house in Silver Lake that seems to be made entirely of windows, with a sandy backyard and two spare rooms; one of these is empty and the other contains a blue foldout couch. Scott assumes that the empty room is earmarked for a child but thinks of the other as his, though he knows the house only from photographs posted online. He'll probably call them from the road tonight or tomorrow morning. Or maybe he'll just show up.

Now he's standing in his soon-to-be-former bedroom, pushing drawers back in, shutting the closet door, smoothing the top sheet. He doesn't want Ellen to think there's been a burglary or, worse, that he's had another woman in the bed. He wishes that he could somehow be there to explain things to her when she comes home—an absurd thought, but it reminds him that he still hasn't written the note.

He tears a piece of paper off the yellow pad that they keep on the counter for their shopping lists. He writes, "I wasn't ready and am so sorry but swear this will have been the right thing for us." Signs his name way down at the bottom in swift cursive, like he does to endorse checks. Leaves himself space to go back and add "Love" as his closing, but isn't sure whether he should. He knows that he's giving up his right to use that word with regard to Ellen, but doesn't know whether that means that he ought to use it this one last time or if the forfeiture has already taken place.

If not "Love," then what?

But just because there's room for a closing doesn't mean there has to be a closing. He didn't begin with a salutation, after all. "Dear Ellen"—how absurd would *that* be? The letter is held on the table by their little brown pepper mill. Whatever happens next is his fault but not his problem. He may never even know about it, whatever "it" will turn out to have been.

Scott locks the front door. His bowels are twisted in hot knots but he doesn't have to go to the bathroom. Indeed, he's eaten nothing but cigarette smoke all day. He plugs his iPod into the dashboard. He knows that it's stupid to soundtrack his own life by picking a song "for the moment," but can't help himself. Puts on Derek and the Dominos' "Key to the Highway," rolls all his windows down, shuts his cell phone off and tosses it in the glove box, lights a cigarette, puts the car into gear, and then, sobbing freely, inaugurates his long ride south.

Scott drives out of Portland half expecting to crash on the highway. He won't cause the accident but he will deserve to suffer it. He imagines how it will go: a flash or a swerve, a drop in his gut, like when an elevator hiccups, then jump cut—waking up alone in a sunny hospital room or a wailing ambulance or somehow back in Ellen's arms in a body cast or even shipped home to a grave beside his grandparents at New Montefiore, in West Babylon. He believes that the universe will charge him with his crime against Ellen, will confirm to him the value of his actions by making him pay dearly for having taken them. This strikes him as a quintessentially Jewish sentiment. He pounds the steering wheel with the heel of his hand and cries out, "Fuck your ancient law!"

Six hours later, the state line safely behind him, he stops for the night in Yreka—a depressing old mining town in the high beautiful woods near Klamath National Forest. The phone stays off and in the glove box. At the Black Bear Diner he orders the Joe's Hobo Omelette—ham, bacon, *and* sausage. *Fuck your ancient law.* The next morning, he gets up, checks out of the Econo Lodge, goes back to the Black Bear, sits in the same seat as the day before, orders the same omelette plus coffee, then gets back on I-5. He figures he'll drive as far as Sacramento, but then the prospect of an evening in that city seems so grim that he takes the 505 to San Francisco, where he uses the family credit card to check into the Omni Hotel.

The Omni has an air of beleaguered elegance: faded crimson carpets roll down scuffed marble stairs into a lobby full of wing chairs; waxed apples brown in a bronze bowl on a sideboard by the elevators. Scott drowns himself in HBO and room service. He showers with the bathroom door open, eats the five-dollar chocolate bar from the minifridge. Through the smoke coat on his tongue, the taste of the bittersweet confection is like glimpsing a hooded figure through swirling fog.

When he turns his phone back on, he learns that Ellen called him sixteen times in the first two days he was gone. Her initial messages are desperate and imploring—"Baby, whatever I did wrong . . ."; "Baby, I don't understand"; "Baby, TALK TO ME"—but that tone is soon supplanted by frustration, then rage. "You pussy!" she screams in one of them. He has never heard her speak this word before, and it pops in his ear like a cold wet finger, sending gooseflesh up his arms and a shiver through his loins. Scott has been at the hotel for a week.

There are also livid messages from his parents, who say that if they don't hear from him within twenty-four hours they will cancel the credit card and hire a private detective. (Empty threats since he hasn't lost the room.) Danny, a college friend who also lives in Portland, sent this text: "You fucking moron, how is she supposed to do anything without a fucking car?"

Scott feels bad about the car. He had thought about it only in terms of ownership, and in doing so failed to consider the question of use. The house that he and Ellen sublet is in a suburb a half hour's drive from her office, from all the good bars, from anywhere she might actually want to be in Portland. He writes back to Danny, "Shit im sorry do u think i should send her $ for a rental?" Danny's reply comes faster than Scott would have guessed it was possible to type on a touch-screen keypad: "FUCK YOU DON'T EVER EVEN THINK HER NAME EVER AGAIN YOU FUCK."

On the phone, he prevails upon Priscilla to sort things out with their folks. She's his ambassador to the family and seems to enjoy the role. She tells him that she and their mother, appalled, have been in touch with Ellen. Their father has been heard to question Scott's honor. "Remind them that Ellen wasn't Jewish," he says to her, wishing he could evict the hint of whine from his voice. He's sitting on the room's windowsill, cigarette on his lip, staring blankly at the office building across the street, itself essentially a blank.

"Believe me, little brother," Priscilla says, "Mom and Dad have *never* needed to be reminded of that."

Scott takes a daily walk through Chinatown. It gets him out of his room for an hour, ensures that he sees the sun—when there is sun to be seen in San Francisco—and keeps him from ordering the same ham-and-Swiss from room service three times a day. In Portsmouth Square Plaza, old men play Chinese chess on stone benches while the wind whips crazily and vagrants pull deposit bottles out of the trash. In the open-faced souvenir shops that line the steep streets there are countless jade or wood statu-ettes of Hotei Buddha, fat and laughing, and sweaters, sweat-shirts, hoodies, and hats in every color of the rayon rainbow, all emblazoned with a Golden Gate Bridge. Scott remembers once having been told that the bridge never stops being painted. They start at one end, and it takes the whole year to get to the other, by which time the old work has absorbed so much dirt and damage that it needs to be redone, and so they begin again.

Sometimes he has lunch at this Japanese place where there is a moat built into the sushi bar. Little blue boats putter along in three inches of water, each tied to the next with shoelace rig-ging, like parading elephants twined trunk to tail. There was a place like this in Portland, but instead of boats it was an electric train set.

Scott orders iced watermelon juice and starts grabbing at the plastic plates that rest on the boats, on which pieces of sushi are grouped in twos and threes. A laminated placemat explains that the pattern of the plate indicates its price. When he's finished eating, a waiter will tally up the plates and give him a bill. He has to be careful when reaching for the plates so that he doesn't bump a boat and send water sloshing up onto it, or else knock the food overboard. The placemat concludes with this terse warning: SINK SAME AS EAT YOU PAY.

Scott never makes it to LA. He takes some money out of his trust to cover first, last, and security on an apartment in the Mission, plus furniture and whatever else he needs: towels, rugs, a bed. He goes on a few dates with a cute barista named Olivia. She has this staggering Afro that she keeps kerchiefed down while she's at work. Scott tells his sister all about her, keeping only two facts from his account: first, that they are not a serious couple; second, that while Olivia is half black she is also half Jewish. On her mother's side, no less. Olivia wasn't bat mitzvahed, but she spits fire if she sees a FREE PALESTINE patch on a backpack. She wants to take one of those birthright trips to Israel to explore her roots. She encourages Scott to take one, too, but stops short of suggesting that they go together. Scott makes his sister understand that Olivia is the first significant girl after Ellen, and so Priscilla tells their mother, and now it's a family scandal. These poor narrow-minded, well-meaning Long Island racists! All this tribal madness about bloodlines, purity—obsessions that have never worked out especially well for Jews. Unless you count the six thousand years of survival (that's what Olivia would say), but then what about, for example, Tay-Sachs? Anyway, he calls home more often. The perplexed suffering in his mother's voice is not unwelcome. He's pretty sure "schvartzeh" is the only Yiddish word his father knows.

On a walk through his new neighborhood, Scott sees a home-made flyer stapled to a utility pole: I FOUND YOUR DOG. There's a photograph of a blond mutt relaxing, stretched out on the floor with its muzzle on its front paws. It looks to be part retriever. Scott takes the flyer down and puts it in his pocket. He calls the number and receives an address, which he plugs into the maps app on his phone. Ten minutes south on the 101 and he's in a part of the city that he's never seen before, a miserable-looking neighborhood below McLaren Park that his phone says is called Sunnydale. The directions lead him to a gravel lot where there are two boxcars.

The boxcars' open doors face each other, and a sun-bleached tarp is secured over the space between them, as an awning; white plastic chairs and a card table suggest a porch. A man with a white beard halfway down his gut and white hair all the way down his back emerges from one car, leaning on a hand-carved walking stick. "You must be who called," the overgrown gnome says.

The boxcars are wired for electricity. The man has three computers going at once. Two of them mine bitcoins, he says, while the third donates its processing power to SETI. "Also grow," he says, gesturing with his stave in the direction of the other boxcar. "Real good shit, if you're interested. Medical grade." The blond dog wanders out from a shadow and comes up to Scott for a sniff. Scott gets down on his knees and opens his arms wide, wondering what the dog will do. It licks his face, so he hugs it. "Found her wandering loose on Dolores," the man says, supplying the story Scott hadn't thought to ask for. "While I was on an, ahem, errand. Hope I didn't cause you too much trouble taking her back here, but I couldn't see leaving her."

Scott produces a bank-crisp hundred-dollar bill from his shirt pocket. The man shakes his head at the money but then takes it anyway. He pounds the ground with his walking stick. "I got a real big heart," he says. "Big enough to burst."

Scott names the dog Yreka. Whenever he walks her, he's on his guard. What if he runs into her original owners? What if they call out to her and she bolts? The dog was found without a collar, and she's put on a healthy amount of weight since Scott brought her home, so the odds are that she was abandoned or neglected. Nonetheless, he can't shake the feeling that he has kidnapped Yreka rather than adopted her, and that somewhere in San Francisco is a person or a couple or a family who miss their dog. They probably live in his neighborhood. Almost every day, he walks by the utility pole where he saw the flyer, and he imagines her owners as a couple, approximately his own age, married a year and a half but childless—like his sister and her husband, they're taking things slow. Before losing her, perhaps they joked that the dog was their trial-run baby. They probably don't make that joke anymore.

Scott names the couple Nate and Jennifer. She's Korean American, born here to immigrant parents, grew up in Foster City. Nate's from Ohio, near Schmall, the town that shares its name with the private college where Scott and Ellen met. Surely Nate didn't attend Schmall, but he probably went to the parties. Maybe he and Scott waited in line for a keg together, made eyes at the same wobbling girl. Maybe Nate even hooked up with Ellen. All the college girls went through a townie phase. Sometimes, when Nate is making his regular love to Jennifer, with her smooth skin and soft belly and perfectly black hair, his mind wanders back to the old days, when a random Thursday night might have delivered him a freckled brunette in a scoop-necked shirt to make love to—where? In somebody's upstairs bathroom or on a back deck, his own childhood bed or Ellen's dorm bed, the woods behind a tumbledown barn.

Scott writes a check for three thousand dollars, leaves the "to" line blank, and folds it into his wallet. If he is ever stopped on the street by the dog's original owners, he will look them in the eye, tell them the plain truth, and offer the check. He will put his palms up and let the leash go free. It will be their choice: the dog or the money. And no matter what happens next, he will at least know Yreka's true name.

Scott and Yreka stop by the coffee shop on their way to Dolores Park, where people lay out blankets on the sunward slope of the great green hill. Olivia gives him a free coffee and a quick kiss on the mouth, then kneels down to ruff up Yreka's fur and kiss her on her cold black nose. She says that she'll be off in an hour and will meet up with them. She disappears into the employee restroom to wash her hands before she makes another drink.

At the vet's office, Scott writes on the form that Yreka is a recent adoptee, that he found her wandering with no collar on Jack Kerouac Alley next to City Lights and brought her home. The vet is happy to report that Yreka is worm free. Also, she's pregnant. He gives Scott a brochure about what to expect. When

Scott gets home, he gives Yreka two extra Beggin' Strips, fishes the unaddressed check from his wallet, and tears it in half. He halves the halves, then repeats this procedure until tiny pale-blue squares burst from his fingers like confetti.

When Scott first got to town, and even after he decided to stay, he held off on getting in touch with any of his contacts in the music scene. But now that he's ready to play shows again it only takes a couple of emails to line up a gig. He's got his headphones plugged into his laptop and his iTunes on shuffle while Yreka snoozes on the couch beside him. He strokes her blond zeppelin belly with one hand while cruising Facebook with the other. He one-hand-types Ellen's full name into the search bar, and when her profile pops up he is astonished to see that she never unfriended him.

Probably she forgot, is all, or else the thought never crossed her mind. Ellen was always an intermittent Facebooker. She isn't one of those people who feel the need to broadcast all the excruciating minutiae of their lives. He reads through her old updates, starting with the day after he left and working his way back to the present. There's not much there: a handful of promo posts for the film festival in the weeks leading up to it, a couple of embedded music videos, a link to a *Times* op-ed about peak oil, a little gallery of photographs from the festival's after-party. He lingers on a snapshot of Ellen, drink-flushed and grinning, her arm around a bemused-looking Gus Van Sant. Her most recent status update is from last week, and all it says is "Ff-frrryyydddaaayyy." Five people "like" this—Percy Tomlinson,

Kat Stokes, Rachel Duncan, Ellen's great-aunt Marlene, and Danny Kramer, the guy who sent Scott the text message warning him never to even think Ellen's name ever again. Scott clicks on Danny's name and is unsurprised to see that Danny *did* unfriend him, which means the only parts of Danny's profile he can see are those few tidbits that he leaves public:

Danny Kramer
Networks: Schmall College; Edgewater High School, Orlando, FL
Music: Rilo Kiley, Wilco, Weezer (only *Pinkerton*—obvs), Neutral Milk Hotel, Mountain Goats, Hank Williams, Velvet Underground
Employers: Not if I can help it.

Danny's profile picture is a close-up of him and Ellen in a staring contest, eyes wide open and nose tips touching, in what Scott believes to be the master bedroom of the house he fled.

Scott's DJ set is totally killer and he knows it. Sweat streaming down his bald head, the firm clamp of the headphones over his ears—he's entering that zone where he's both more and less himself than any other time: he is everyone dancing in the whole hot venue, and he's the huge amps hung on shining chains from the black ceiling, and he's the thunder being flung from the amps' blind mesh faces. He's all of it at once but also none of it—beautifully, perfectly, inexhaustibly nothing at all.

Olivia comes over to him while he's packing up, a rocks glass in each hand.

"Nice set," she says, grinning. She nods at his equipment case. "Nice gear, too."

"Medical grade," he says, giving her the same nod back. "One of those for me?"

"That depends."

"On what?"

"Oh, I'll let you know," she says, and then they're both laughing. Then they've finished their Jamesons, and he's loading his gear into his trunk while she orders them another round. When the next DJ goes on, Scott pulls Olivia out onto the dance floor. The whole rest of the perfect night the lightning of success is wild in him—through the next set and last call and the smeary, invincible drunk drive home. Then they're somehow in his room, and here's his tall girlfriend on her naked knees as he explodes across her tits and chin.

They lie on their backs, breathing deep and slow in the hot dark. Scott realizes that the universe is ungoverned: there is no law for him to be an outlaw from. He says to Olivia that he's going to take the dog out for a walk. She tells him not to be long. He throws on the shirt that he was wearing earlier and a pair of jeans without underwear. He enters the living room on watery legs and flips the light on. Yreka, surprised by the sudden burst of light, whimpers pitifully but does not pause in her effort to eat her newest whelp free from its amniotic sac. If she doesn't hurry, it will drown in there, and the next one is already on its way—a shiny purple oval like an enormous cold-medicine capsule or a small translucent dinosaur egg inching out of her distended vulva. The couch, of course, is ruined. Inside the emergent sac is something like a bald rabbit trapped in gelatin: squirming, blind, awake.

Olivia, naked in the bedroom doorway, draws a sharp breath when she sees why Scott is frozen. She sidles up behind him, her belly against his back, and slides her arms around his waist—thumbs hooked into the belt loops of his jeans. Yreka licks her chops, then grabs her youngest pup by the scruff. She plunks it over by its brothers and sisters, four—now five—wrinkled pink things mewling in residual slime. By the time it's over, Yreka has whelped nine puppies. Scott knows from the brochure to expect to lose a few of these, but there's no apparent runt, and by the evening of the next day it's clear that the whole litter will survive. Life becomes a blur of tiny bodies in harmless cease-less collision. Mouths yip and teeth nip and new claws emerge and scratch. The living room is transformed into a nursery, and the whole apartment stinks of shit and newspapers. Yreka's teats bleed from the rough, unending attention: her blond muzzle shows its first threads of white, tired pride now inscribed in her watery wise brown eyes. Scott loves the puppies but doesn't know how he would have managed without Olivia. She's over at his place so often he winds up making her a key.

MIKE'S SONG

Mike Beckstein's in his kitchen, sitting at the small round table, drinking a glass of organic, pulp-free orange juice, idly regarding but not precisely looking at his MacBook. Ken and Angie, his grown son and daughter, are in their respective childhood bedrooms, going through their closets and drawers. It's the last week of December—and good riddance, as far as Mike's concerned; '09 was a shit year. Come spring he and Miranda are selling the place—thus completing, finally, their divorce settlement—so the kids have to decide what's important enough to keep and what can be thrown away, which so far seems to be pretty much everything.

There are three tabs open in Firefox and a to-do list in an unsaved Word doc. Behind those windows, and therefore at the moment entirely hidden from view, his desktop wallpaper is a photo from the 2007 Masters of himself with defending champ

Phil Mickelson—who later that same day would surprise everyone by blowing his opening rounds and nearly getting cut.

Ken, shouting down the hallway: "Why does every trip
down memory lane seem to end at the city dump?"

Angie, calling back to her brother: "Maybe if American
childhood consisted of more than collecting every last Beanie
Baby and fucking baseball card . . ." This comment not explicitly a dig at Mike—though not explicitly not a dig either—just
the words of a hard-nosed progressive reduced by present circumstance to her inner pissed-off teen. And it's true that the
only thing the kids remember about most of this stuff is buying
it: the jolt of commercial desire followed by the soft shock of success as the parental wallet opened—and then the getting bored.
A long day of Internet price checking—Mike's job, hence the
tabs and list—has yielded little. All this stuff really is junk: the
small black-eyed bears forlorn in their Ziploc baggies; a Mike
Piazza rookie in a plastic screw case; all five installments of DC
Comics's "limited edition" Zero Hour series, each issue in its
own polymer sleeve with white cardboard backer. The complete
set, mint condition, on eBay right now, is going for ten bucks.
Now the Piazza card, on the other hand, might have been worth
some real cash if it had been mint—and a Bowman instead of a
Fleer, but what can you do? Not like they need the money. But it
would've been—what? Validating, somehow, and a nice surprise
if even one of these things had paid out.

Anyway, it's about time to knock off and hit the road.
They've got tickets to go see the kids' favorite group, the Phish,
play the first of four concerts at the Miami Arena—technically

American Airlines Arena now, but Mike prefers the old name, just as he'll always think of the stadium where the Dolphins play as Joe Robbie, not Pro Player or Sun Life or whoever owns the naming rights for next year.

Angie—who lives in Brooklyn—insists that she be the one to drive. "Gotta get the practice when I can," she says, and Mike could make this into a thing about how if she came home to visit more she would have more chances, etc., but that's one conversation he doesn't want to get into without an exit strategy, besides which she's not wrong about the practice thing, so here he is riding shotgun in his own champagne-colored Saab.

Ken says he doesn't mind sitting in back.

Mike, catching a glimpse of himself in the side-view mirror, stops to take a good long look: close-cropped salt-and-pepper hair—well, mostly salt these days, but still thick, and wavy if he'd ever let it grow out; nose getting a little bulbous, old-man-ly; not too many lines on his face at least, except around his eyes or when he smiles wide, a rare enough occurrence; the eyes themselves pale blue and chilly, almost alien, exuding calm power. Self-assurance. A self-made man. A wealthy man. A real estate lawyer, B.S.D. at a premier firm, with two grown children who have largely forgiven what he did to their mother, wearing a two-hundred-dollar knit pullover with the sleeves pushed up to the elbows, a modest gold link bracelet on the wrist of one hairy well-toned arm.

This used to be an open neighborhood, but a couple years ago the community board got a measure through the city council to wall it off and put up a guard gate—inconvenient, but great for property values—which means there's only one way in and out, which means that Angie will have to drive past the old Rosen house, which happens to be on the street where the gate is. Mike himself drives past it every day, so it's no big deal to him. But the kids? They were fifteen and sixteen when Brad—a neighborhood boy, Ken was friendly with him—cut his own throat in his backyard with a kitchen knife. There was more to it than that, but the details are vague to Mike now. An article in the *Herald* had speculated about a "black magic" angle, that the kid had been attempting some kind of heavy metal voodoo Satanist—well, he doesn't remember what the claims were, and anyway that's all they ever were: Claims. Rumors. Busybody chatter. Some hack columnist clawing his way onto A1. One line from the piece that's always stuck with Mike: "A stunning tragedy that has shaken this close-knit, well-off community to its core." Not to suggest that Mike thinks money can stop bad things from happening, but in his heart of hearts he might believe it should.

Ken is twenty-five now; Angie's twenty-six. They're what in the old days were called Irish twins—eleven months between them, though they were a grade apart all through school, which Mike believes was for the best. Their mother was less sure. Where Mike always feared the kids in competition, Miranda saw lost opportunities for camaraderie. Doing their homework together, standing up for each other. All water under the bridge now, ancient history, dust in the wind—Mike tries to think of another cliché and can't. No matter, point's made, and all that stuff about Brad Rosen is no less ancient, no less blown away.

"So you guys psyched for the Phish?" Mike asks.

"It's 'Phish,' Dad, not 'the Phish.'" That's Angie chiding him. How many years have they been correcting him about this and it still won't stick?

"He does it just to bug you," Ken says from the backseat. Mike smiles and shrugs noncommittally. It's not true, what Ken said, but he likes the idea. Ken and Angie love their Phish like they love few other things in this world. He likes them himself, well enough anyway, not that he ever plays their music at home. What he likes is seeing his kids together, enjoying each other's company, sharing a common interest—all that hokey shit that when you get right down to it really and truly is what it's all about. Family time's not been easy to come by of late. Mike knows he's not blameless, as far as that goes, but he also doesn't blame himself for taking what he can get—these primo tickets, for example, the way he dangled them out before his kids like fruit. They spent Thanksgiving with their mother in Tampa so they'd be free to spend New Year's week with him.

They're passing the house now, though the Rosens them-selves haven't lived there in—he isn't sure of that either, but let's say nine years. Nobody says anything but the kids' heads both turn so Mike looks, too, though at first he's looking at them looking rather than at the house itself. The living room cur-tains are open and the lights are on. People sitting at a table in the dining room, two adults and two kids: a girl who might be seven and a bibbed toddler wriggling in a booster seat. Through a doorway on the right side of the dining room you can see into the kitchen with its small round table. It occurs to Mike that the floor plan of the Rosen house is a mirror image of his own house. Which is itself truly nothing special since every house in the neighborhood is one of four designs (eight with the reversed versions included) but still—to have never noticed such a thing before.

"Do you think they know about what happened?" Ken asks.

"Jesus Christ," Angie says. "Why would you even ask that?"

"I'm sure it came up when they were negotiating, if not sooner," Mike says. He's about to start ballparking what it probably cost the Rosens, in terms of resale value, when Angie says, "Please, for fuck's sake, can we just, like, not?"

She slows toward the guard gate, not quite needing to come to a complete stop before the sensor reads the beige plastic card clipped to the sun visor. The gate arm—a white plank of wood striped with orange reflective tape—eases itself skyward and they coast on through. Then it's a quick right onto the I-95 overpass, then the loop-around on-ramp for the southbound lanes. In the car there's no noise but the white rush of the air conditioner and the thrum of their wheels on the road.

"Hey, so why don't we put some tunes on?" Mike says. The sooner this silence is broken, he feels, the better. Ken reaches through the space between the front seats and plugs a thin black cord into a jack on the dashboard. Now he can DJ off his iPhone. Mike pays both kids' phone bills because it's a better value, he says, for them to all be on a family plan. Angie used to insist on sending Mike a check every month for her share, but he never cashed them and eventually she stopped.

"Here's a great version of my song from '98," Ken says, stringy hair falling in his face as he stares at the glowing rectangle, scrolling through MP3s with a swerve of his thumb. "They're gonna play it tonight—second set opener, I can feel it."

"Nah, they'll save it for New Year's Eve," Angie says.

"Could be both," Ken says, "but tonight for sure."

"How can you possibly know that?" Angie's getting exasperated; when it comes to her brother, it doesn't take a lot.

"Sister, I can feel it in my bones."

"What makes it 'your song,' Ken?" Mike interjects, hoping to head off this argument before it can get going.

"Not 'my,' Dad," Angie says, replying on her brother's behalf. "'Mike's.' It's called 'Mike's Song.' So I guess it's yours if it's anybody's." She laughs.

"Well, yours and Mike Gordon's," Ken adds. Mike knows enough to know that Mike Gordon is the bass player. He could ask for more details but doesn't want a full-blown history lesson. When Ken gets going about the Phish, forget it.

"I guess we'll have to share then," Mike says, forcing a laugh of his own. He hates when he's wrong about things. Ken hits the play button and music fills the car. Mike recognizes the little signature of notes that kicks the song off—he just never knew its name before and hadn't thought to ask. It's six o'clock on a weeknight but all the traffic's headed in the other direction. Already dark out. They're making great time.

He takes his own phone out of his pocket and knocks out a quick text to Lori—"Thinking of you, cannot wait until nye, xo"—but then he doesn't send it, instead goes back and changes

"Thinking" to "thinkin"; "cannot" to "cant," though the auto-correct grants him the apostrophe; "you" to "u"; and finally, in place of the "xo," an animated smiley face that will wink at her when she opens the message. Ken and Angie are going back on the thirty-first for the New Year's Eve show; Lori and Mike, who haven't seen each other much this week, are going to spend the night alone. He's got a bottle of Rías Baixas that's going to be perfect with the steak she's planning to make them. Music on the stereo, the countdown on the living room TV.

"Who you talking to, Dad?" Angie asks.

"Just Barry," Mike says.

"Oh."

Barry Stern's another rainmaker at the firm and at this point Mike's oldest, closest friend. He's someone about whom Angie will have no further questions, especially since he's currently going through a nasty divorce himself, which she will definitely not want to hear about, or else has already heard about from their mother, who would have given Christina's version, not that Mike's got anything to say in his friend's defense. Barry was always a fuck-around, but then he started getting reckless, and since having been kicked out of the house he's been on an almost nihilistic tear—secretaries, summer associates, maybe one of the interns (Mike isn't certain and doesn't want to know); he's going to get the shit kicked or sued out of him one of these days, maybe both. Not that anyone else would see it this way, but compared to Barry, Mike's been practically a saint. He rarely stepped out on Miranda, and when he did it was only ever with professionals. You're in town somewhere a few days on business, let's say, and you've been given a number by someone you trust. You call the number and that's that. Or you're sitting at a titty bar and the dancer leans in close and whispers that she's about to get off her shift. He was safe and discreet about all of it. This thing with Lori was a total surprise.

The kids know Lori exists but they haven't met her. A picture of her on the fridge has gone thus far unremarked. He thought about inviting her out tonight but wasn't sure how they would have reacted to the proposal, and his instinct said to let things lie for the time being, besides which Lori didn't want to see Phish, though that hasn't stopped her from acting hurt about being, quote, "left out." "I'm sure we'd have tons in common," she'd said of his children. "Being the same age and all." Which isn't true—Lori's almost thirty-two—but close enough to make Mike certain that delaying introductions was the right move. One ancillary benefit of this plan is he'll spare himself seeing whatever shit shape Ken's bound to be in by the time the New Year's concert lets out. Another good reason for letting Angie get her driving practice in tonight.

Angie. He looks at his daughter, appraising: she was a blond baby, now a chestnut-haired woman with his chilly eyes—green, like her mother's, but still, indubitably, his. Sturdy close eyebrows, thin lips, no makeup, a sharpness to her jawline that makes her face seem to taper toward an almost heart-like chin. A beautiful woman in black jeans and a pale-yellow T-shirt, her slender fingers drumming the steering wheel, her face flashing in and out of shadow as they fly through the night.

She was always the precocious one, a pain in the ass some-times but easy to be proud of. Great grades in school even when she was in her "rebellious" phase, partial scholarship to NYU, internships every summer; always in a rush to get her life started, to be the best. She works for a feminist nonprofit—something like Emily's List but not Emily's List—urging rich old Democrat ladies to support city council and statehouse can-didates. When Mike and Miranda wanted to see her they'd go to New York, which wasn't a bad arrangement by any means: breeze in, try out whichever new hotel Mike had been hearing about, museum and a Mets game, Broadway show if there was anything decent playing, hugs and kisses and a town car back to JFK. Which is still pretty much how the visits go, come to think of it, only Angie hasn't invited him in a while, and the next time he goes it will probably be alone.

Ken's had a more difficult time than his sister in terms of, let's say, finding himself, and even that's a charitable way of put-ting it—but why shouldn't Mike show his own kid some char-ity? He's rocking out in the backseat, head bopping, eyes closed, hollow-cheeked and vaguely horsey with a weak goatee. Faded red corduroys and a blue T-shirt commemorating some other Phish concert he went to six years ago. A hemp necklace strung with a single ceramic bead the color of river mud. Ken's a guitar player, and quite gifted, which Mike's not saying merely as the boy's father but rather as a man who prides himself on knowing shit from Shinola. When Ken finished high school he stayed right on living at home, enrolled at Miami-Dade Community College, worked part-time at a restaurant in the mall. Turned out he didn't like restaurant work much, or community college, so the next year he transferred up to FSU, which it turned out he didn't like either, though he still lives in Tallahassee; when pressed he says he'll go back to school sooner or later, "when the time's right." Meanwhile he seems to be doing okay living off his music (plus a not-inconsiderable monthly supplement from Mike), playing at bars by the college and at house parties, jamming on the side with a couple guys who tour with George Clinton. He's never met Clinton himself but says there's been some talk that if a spot ever opens up he'd almost definitely get asked to audition. Anyway, he's still finding himself.

Mike envies musicians, and has always talked about trying to learn, but he's always sort of known he'd never do it, and indeed he never has, which may explain why he cuts his son so much slack to be a slacker with—because he would rather view himself as indulgent than jealous. Mike knew Ken would come for the holidays. And knows that he'll stay longer than originally planned, in no rush to make the long drive back upstate, grateful for access to a stocked fridge and free laundry. Angie, on the other hand—well, Mike doubts she'd even be here if not for the concerts. She's leaving on New Year's Day, the earliest flight she could get. So maybe he'll introduce Lori to Ken next week at some point, like a test case, and if that goes well then Ken can sort of help soften his sister up about the whole situation and maybe next time it can be all of them together. If nothing else, the band's bound to come through town again.

Which is funny, when Mike thinks about it, because when Angie was younger she hated the Phish like they were poison, dog shit, lepers, the scum of the earth. He'd forgotten about this but now, in the car, he remembers. The kids used to fight about music like it was some kind of religious schism. Which in truth is probably exactly what it seemed like from their perspectives at the time, Mike realizes, remembering a screaming match he once had with his father about a Jimi Hendrix record. Kids! Mike remembers Angie and her fat friend—what was her name?—the miserable girl who used to be over at the house all the time playing records by that Marilyn Manson, teaching Angie to wear fishnets and powder her face pale so she looked like a dead hooker—Dawn! Dawn was the fat girl's name. Angie and Dawn used to cover their ears and scowl whenever Ken put his "hippie" music on. They'd run shrieking across the house to Angie's room and slam the door. God how Mike had hated Marilyn shit-ass Manson. Would've liked to ban all that crap from his house, and probably would have, only Miranda believed in letting kids test boundaries, express themselves, whatever. Whatever the fuck Miranda had believed. But time heals all wounds, doesn't it? Nobody thinks about Marilyn shit-ass Manson anymore, while Hendrix is still very much a god. Ken says the Phish sometimes cover "Bold as Love" in their encore. Mike's got his fingers crossed.

Mike is about to ask Angie whatever happened with Dawn, but then thinks better of it. He seems to remember that the friendship ended abruptly—one day Dawn was a fixture in Angie's life and then one day she wasn't, and if he ever asked about it at the time he was surely rewarded with rolled eyes and frosty silence. Teenagers. And come to think of it, wasn't Brad Rosen sometimes hanging around too in those days? Mike doesn't remember the boy so much as he does his own annoyance, still visceral even at this late remove, at coming home from a punishing day at the office to a house full of other people's kids. Miranda on the phone with the pizza guy, shrugging her shoulders as in, What can you do? Then one day Brad Rosen up and kills himself and Dawn stops coming around.

Angie eases the Saab into the exit lane. They pass below the monorail track, looking for a decent place to park. There's something ominous about downtown Miami, an abandoned feeling even on streets where the city's renaissance (Angie calls it "gentrification") is in full swing. Not that this, where they are now, is one of those streets. Nobody's on the sidewalk; a streetlight's out. All the stores have Spanish signage and their metal gates down. Angie sees an open spot but Mike says to keep going.

They end up paying twenty-eight dollars to park in the garage at the Bayside Mall, conveniently adjacent to the arena, though Ken says they've got to "scope the lot scene" before they go inside.

Grilled cheese and veggie burritos cooking up on portable griddles set on truck beds and station wagon gates. Dreadheaded guys in hoodies all over the place; Ken says half of them are cops. He's on the lookout for a friend of his—this guy Adam from their high school, doesn't Angie remember, he was in her grade—still nothing? Oh well.

A minute later a voice says, "Hey, whoa, meet the Becksteins!"

"Adam! Dude!" Ken and the guy embrace. Mike and Angie watch. Adam gives Angie a quick hug during which her arms remain firmly at her sides; then he shakes Mike's hand. The kid's wearing brown cargo shorts and skateboard shoes and an old holey T-shirt that identifies him as a staff member of a JCC youth camp in the summer of 1998, the same year as the "Mike's Song" they listened to in the car, which Ken—staunch believer in omens—will certainly take for a promising sign if he notices.

"Hey, we'll be right back," Ken says. "Adam's got some, uh, bootlegs in his car I want to see."

"Right," Angie says. "We'll be over there." She points down the row of parked cars to where two guys with guitars and a girl with a tambourine are giving an impromptu performance, playing acoustic covers of songs they're hoping to hear tonight. Mike and Angie stand near enough to hear them but not so close as to make eye contact, perchance to be obliged to throw a bill into the guitar case open like a mouth at the players' feet. Mike taps his own foot in time with the music, steals a glance at his phone.

Should he send Lori another message? He'd like to. But how many sweet nothings should you have to whisper before you get one back? He puts the phone away. It hasn't been that long. Better to play it cool. *Get it together, Mike, you fucking pussy.* That's what Barry would say.

Ken comes back empty-handed.

"Nothing you liked?" Mike asks. At first his son doesn't seem to have understood the question, but then he snaps to something like attention.

"Oh yeah, well, I heard all those shows before."

Angie guffaws. Everyone in the lot seems to be selling something: stickers, T-shirts, necklaces, glass pipes packed in custom foam cases or laid out loose on black cloths in the dirt. They can hear the hiss of a nitrous tank somewhere nearby but out of sight. A wide-eyed girl with hairy armpits and acne around her mouth walks past them, mumbling in singsong, "Goo balls, goo balls."

Ken looks at his family. "I'd split one," he says, in a tone perfectly calibrated to make it unclear which one of them he's talking to or whether he's even serious.

"Your friend didn't want to walk in with us?" Angie asks.

"He doesn't have a ticket."

"No ticket? Gee, then what's he doing here?"

"Waiting for a miracle, I guess."

They leave the lot and head inside, make their way through the bottleneck at security, then get in an all-things-considered-not-too-terribly-bad line to buy foamy beers that cost eleven dollars apiece. Their seats are down on the floor, twenty rows back from the stage. You wouldn't believe what these tickets cost. And the ones for New Year's Eve? Forget it. A roar sweeps the audience as the house lights go down.

They open with a song Mike recognizes but can't name. It's got slowish verses that build toward this quasi-anthemic chorus that the whole crowd shouts along with. Ken produces a joint from somewhere on his person, lights it, puffs twice, then offers it to his sister. Mike is determined to be unsurprised no matter what his daughter does, but he doesn't try to hide his curiosity— he's staring at her, waiting to see. She only takes one toke, but it's a good toke, then offers the joint to Mike. She's holding her hand out but avoiding looking him in the eye—apparently unsure herself about what reaction to expect, but Mike made his decision about this earlier and so takes it without hesitation. Miranda will shit fire if she ever finds out—which fact he will remind his kids of, if and when he ever feels the need to play a card. Mike makes sure his toke is as long as his daughter's. He hacks into his fist, then tokes again.

Songs come and go. One opens with this long, sinuous guitar part that feels like walking through a curving tunnel and suspecting that the trail is doubling back on itself but not being sure. Then in a later part of the same song—he thinks it's the same song, at any rate—there are these intervals where the band stops playing for two beats while the whole audience does these handclaps and then there's this kind of chanting-wailing part—who knows what babble the lyrics are?—but then the lead singer's voice is suddenly clear as a bell and he's asking, hardly singing now, more like shouting, "Was it for this my life I sought?" and twenty-some-odd thousand people shout back at him, "Maybe so and maybe not!" Mike watches Ken, fist pumping in rhythm with the chant, screaming with what seems to be conviction. Mike can't remember the last time he saw his son so excited about anything. Figures that the one thing that does it for him would be a declaration of existential uncertainty.

The guitar solo takes off like a bird, no, like a flock of birds, and Mike's mind is adrift in the music, then away from it, the remainder of the set passing by as he thinks about a leather couch he saw at West Elm that he's going to get for the condo he's going to get after he unloads the house. Lori went with him and helped pick it out—the couch that is, though she's also gone with him to see a number of properties. He's almost made up his mind. Lori. Her downy face, wet eyes the same warm brown as the roots she lets show beneath her shock-blond hair. She likes smock blouses and matchstick jeans. Her favorite color is aquamarine. They met at a party on Mike's friend's yacht. She was pale in her bikini, somebody's wife's niece, drinking a screwdriver and standing alone. He imagines her in his new condo, a high-rise on the beach or pretty near it: A marble breakfast bar separates the living room from the kitchen, the leather couch they picked out sitting opposite a wall-mounted flat-panel TV. She's in the kitchen in the morning in her panties and an unbuttoned shirt of his, rinsing the dregs of last night's wine from a long-stemmed glass.

The ending of a song snaps him back to reality. The band starts up a new song but then they interrupt themselves a minute in so the lead singer can tell some kind of story while the drummer climbs out from behind his kit. It is revealed that the drummer is going to "play" a vacuum cleaner by sticking his face up to the hose part and letting it suck on his lips. Mike remembers teenage Ken raving about how cool it was that they did stuff like this; Mike himself always thought it sounded like second-rate Zappa gags and, seeing it live, now feels retroactively validated. The drummer is wearing a sleeveless polka-dot muumuu. The vacuum makes a sound like a dentist's drill. When it's over they play a couple more normal songs to close out the set.

The house lights go up and Angie says she's going to go find the bathroom. Mike gives her forty bucks and tells her to pick up another round of beers on her way back. Mike watches Ken staring glassy-eyed at the empty stage. Christ, Ken. His long hair's in a tight ponytail, fixed with an elastic band he borrowed from his sister; his pupils are like pits in the earth. Mike can see that Ken's hair is starting to thin in front. Soon enough it'll start to pull back. Mike's never had much cause to think about this sort of thing. The men in his family do not, as a rule, go bald. This is the opposite of Miranda's family—her father, her brother, all her uncles bare up top like someone reached in with an ice cream scoop. "Scalped," Miranda's brother, Derek, used to say with a laugh. Probably still says—just not to Mike. And baldness travels on the maternal gene, so that'll be Ken before his thirtieth birthday, and it's all his wife's fault, and for once he'd like to say that out loud, fucking scream it, as if volume were the arbiter of truth, which, come to think of it, always has been the secret message of rock and roll. That and, of course, Never get old.

"Hey, Ken," Mike says. "Can I ask you something?" No response. He tries again: "Ken."

"Oh, hey, Dad, sorry, spaced there. Wassup?"

"Nothing, nothing. I just, well, I was wondering, do you know why Angie got so upset when you mentioned Brad?"

"Yeah, sorry, I shouldn't have done that."

"But why? He was *your* friend, wasn't he?"

"I mean I guess so. But he tried to kiss her once, like not that long before he, you know."

"I never knew that."

"Well, duh, of course not. You're the *dad*, Dad. I shouldn't have said anything. I mean I wouldn't have, normally, but I'm pretty—" He stops himself short, looks away from Mike, and wiggles his fingers stageward; this gesture, apparently, meant to complete the sentence.

"Hey, guys." Angie's back with the beers. She hands Mike his drink, which he takes, and his change, seven bucks, which he refuses. He tells her to put some gas in the car on the thirty-first. She shrugs and pockets the money. Ken raises his cup up and the other two move to meet his cheers.

"But what are we drinking to?" Ken asks.

"It's your cheers," Angie says.

"Shit, I dunno."

"To new beginnings in the new year," offers Mike.

"Sláinte!" Ken says, happy, his unsteady hand sloshing foam onto the floor. Angie stops her cup a moment shy of contact, deftly reverses course, takes a long drink instead. Mike feels his jaw clench. The house lights, mercifully, go down.

First song of the second set it happens: the guitar serves up that signature volley of notes that they heard in the car. Mike can almost see the smooth lines arcing through the air, like when you're signing a contract and it feels like the pen has your name coiled up inside it and all you need to do is set it free. The stage lights turn the whole arena ocean-green and Ken's on his feet, tiptoes even, doing a double fist pump, his instincts and faith in the world affirmed. Angie leans over, her rebuke to him from a moment ago already ancient history, forgotten; she's wearing a grin about a mile wide now, shouting into Mike's ear, "Dad! It's your song, it's your song!" Then she's out of her chair also, arms and hips asway.

"Mike's Song" blurs into the next song and then the next. Mike might be the only person in the whole arena still sitting in his seat. His beer's in one hand, the other hand's in his pocket, tracing a fingertip around the tiny rim of the camera lens built into his phone. He takes his phone out and looks at it. There are three texts from Lori. Three! He thought he'd set the thing to vibrate, but he hadn't, and obviously he wouldn't have heard the incoming-message bleep over the music.

The first message was sent fifteen minutes ago. It says, "hell yea come over im tipsy and undressed."

The second one, sent thirty seconds after the first, says, "Hey shit sorry that was 4 jess. She's with this girl dena we went to school with. Gotta get dressed now obvs hehe. Talk tmrw."

Then, four minutes later: "Hope yr have gr8 nite with yr kids."

Mike closes his fist around the phone, gets out of his seat, makes his way down the row, then the aisle, steps into the hallway, calls her—straight to voicemail. He hangs up on the outgoing message, wishing there were some way to delete the record of his missed call from her log. He goes back inside.

With the encore, set two ends up running about an hour and a half. So the whole show? Let's say three hours. Mike, though long since bored with the music, is impressed by the value the Phish give for the money. He can see why they're so popular; if this was your idea of a great night you'd probably feel like you got everything you came for and more. It's late now. Angie offers to drive home but this time doesn't insist. She lets her brother ride shotgun on account of its being "his turn" but really because she wants to stretch out in the backseat and fall asleep. Ken reclines his own seat, lolls his head back, and soon enough is sleeping, too. They're back on the highway, northbound, the miles rolling by.

Glancing over at his sleeping son, Mike notices the white cap of a prescription canister peeking out of Ken's pocket. He understands immediately that this is what that preshow meet-up with the high school buddy was about. Mike's hands are tight on the steering wheel. He's way over the speed limit. A bead of sweat draws a wet line down the back of his neck. For some reason, Brad Rosen's face appears in his mind then, bright as a firework, clear as a dream: a sallow, sad kid with bad mustache down walking through his mirror-world version of Mike's house, easing the sliding glass door open and slipping out into the yard. He loves Mike's daughter so much he almost hates her. The knife blade catches moonlight when he raises it and there's the red line blooming across his throat, unretractable, blood pouring onto the grass.

Tomorrow Lori will tell him about how good it was to see her old girlfriends; she will roll her eyes while using the word "appletini"; she will be lying to him or telling the truth. He will believe her or not believe her. They will celebrate New Year's Eve. She will lie with her head hanging off the side of the bed so he can watch her finger herself while he fucks her mouth upside down. He'll tell Barry about it and Barry will clap him on the back and tell him next time he ought to take a picture. A few hours later Barry will text him, "was serious btw. got a great little library going. plenty to trade."

Mike takes the off-ramp too fast, barrels hard into the long, tight curve with the wheels sliding beneath him, seeing now how the night will end—his car flipped over on the embankment, lights and sirens swallowing the dark, him and the kids in separate ambulances, in and out of consciousness, Miranda's phone ringing in her kitchen, her blue robe pulled tight around her body as she stumbles half asleep toward the noise—but no, that's not what happens because Mike stays in control, gasses into the turn, the Saab like a part of his body now, an extension of his will as he holds the road and makes it through the loop, straightens out and comes to a stop at the light, where he can take his hands off the wheel and flex them, wipe his forehead and neck, check to see if Ken and Angie have woken, which, thankfully, they haven't, and if he has any luck left they'll stay asleep until he gets them back into their own driveway, where he'll wake them up one at a time, gently, like he used to do when they were kids.

POETS

They met at the mixer the week before their semester started. He seemed ambitious, a pleaser; she walked away annoyed. But it was a small program and she was resigned to running into him in hallways and at events. Perhaps they'd have workshop together. They were poets and this was graduate school.

A computer lab in the basement of their program's building on West 11th Street: grapefruit-colored chairs with screwheads poking through the fabric, the old desktops purring as their cooling fans kicked into gear. She could usually be found there before class, checking her email or some goth band's tour schedule. She was a smart girl but young—fresh out of her undergrad with no "time off" and the city made her feel younger still. Her classmates were mostly in their late twenties, early thirties; some were even older. She was quick to anger and to judge, and knew these things about herself. She had some mastery over her emotions, but it was hard to sustain. Often she did not even try. Dark circles weighted her warm brown eyes; below those, a perfect nose and pout. She drew people's attention but couldn't keep it—or maybe could have but didn't want to. Frequently she herself was uncertain which it was, and refused as a matter of inchoate principle to consider the question at any length. Psychology was for losers! Her name was Abigail Paige. A loner in tight black jeans and fingerless gloves—somehow exquisite in whichever shirt she'd happened to pluck from her bedroom floor that morning—she had a hard, lithe beauty despite greasy hair the color of late wheat.

When Cal came into the lab and Abigail was there he took a station close to hers, the next one over if he could get it. He'd interrupt her to ask how things were going, what was new. She pointedly ignored him but sometimes slipped and gave an answer. He lit up when she did that and she felt a hot, sharp shift inside of herself, like a needle between her guts. Then she'd clam up, furious, as though she'd been taken advantage of in some small but definitive way.

When Abigail came in and Cal was already seated she made a point of sitting far down the row from him, every unoccupied terminal between them another condemnation. But if Cal felt rebuked he did not let on. In a way, she was coming to realize, he was as guarded as she was. He broadcast his pleasantries, kept everything else to the vest. Cal was a wall masquerading as a window. When she sat far away from him in the lab he simply did his work, or whatever it was he was doing, and then when he was finished took a stroll by her station to say hello before he left.

Somewhere early on she told him a lie. It came unprompted, a non sequitur, practically: she said that she had a boyfriend in Baltimore with whom she was quite serious. She said they had been together several years and saw each other as often as they could. He was getting his start down there and who knew but maybe she would ditch New York and poetry school to go be with him. The imaginary boyfriend had a big house in a bad neighborhood, tended an organic garden, played drums. They'd get dogs and take them running. If she went.

Cal was apparently undeterred by this boyfriend. But then, he hadn't declared himself or made a proper move on her either. Was it possible he did just want to be friends? This thought, she found, sent sine waves of dread thrumming up from the base of her spine to the base of her skull. Abigail wanted to be wanted, and to be asked a direct question to which she could reply with an equally direct negation. As in: Fuck you, hopes.

But he didn't ask.

She allowed that he was kind of all right looking. In a way. A little shorter than her—which she liked, actually— and somewhat koala-faced, but with lips so full you could tug them (she guessed) like a dog with a chew toy and needless to say she liked that, too. He looked better when dusted with a few days' stubble, and if he ever let his haircut grow out he would pretty much be there. Artfully ripped blue jeans and vintage shirts made his uniform. It fit. As the chill slid in he layered on cardigans and hoodies. He hated winter coats, he said, and meant to hold out—if possible—until he left for Christmas break.

On New Year's Eve it dipped below zero. She smoked pot alone in her Queens sublet and watched the ball drop on TV, unable to believe her own proximity to where this ritual idiocy was taking place. When her mom called at midnight she was too blitzed to form words so she set the phone to vibrate and watched it jitterbug across the coffee table. She wanted to choose the perfect album to masturbate to, but the studious care she brought to such deliberations quickly lulled her to sleep—clothes on, lights on, stereo still off.

By the time classes resumed in late January she had made up her mind. She was all set to go to the computer room as usual, and what would happen was she would get there second, see where Cal was sitting, and take the station next to his. She'd sit down. He would notice the chair moving in the corner of his eye but wouldn't register the identity of the person. Then, when she was settled, she would turn to him and say hello, and he would understand instantly that things had changed.

Instead they ran into each other in the lobby of the building, the first time such a thing had happened. Cal was in predictably high spirits, smiling. "What's new in Baltimore?" he asked.

"I broke up with that asshole." Abigail practically spit the words at him. The lobby had high ceilings and a bank of windows. Students swirled around them, headed hurriedly to and from. The poetry program met in the evenings. Outside, the day had waned to a dim gray wisp. He hadn't responded to the thing she'd said. What was he waiting for?

"So if you ever want to, you know, hang out." She heard these new words enter the world, spoken in her own voice. After all this time, she had asked him out? She could have slapped him, scratched his eyes from his head, for teasing this out of her.

Oh, but the look on his face was priceless, and Abigail felt with some satisfaction that even though the plan had gone totally FUBAR, the main goal—to turn his world upside down—had still been achieved. "Yeah, I'd like that," he said. "What are you doing after class?"

"I have plans tonight," she said (another lie), "but we could do something Thursday." It was Monday.

"Great," he said. "How about Chinatown?"

"Yeah, Chinatown's cool," she said. And who knew, maybe it was.

They ate soup dumplings and a noodle thing with mushrooms in a brown sauce, and maintained their good cheer even upon learning that the place did not serve hard liquor, only Chinese beer. Afterward, they wandered the chilly, fetid streets until they saw a sports bar on Baxter that would have made more sense in Hell's Kitchen. They ducked in and drank a round; then she said it was getting late and he took out his wallet to pay. They'd split dinner, but he wanted to please at least buy her a drink. There was only one bartender and he had his back turned, down at the far end. It was busy in the place; on the blaring TVs the so-and-sos were up 56–49 over the who-gave-a-shits. She put her hand over his hand. He looked up. She put her lips to his ear. A husky whisper rich with urgency: "C'mon." He furrowed his eyebrows; she kept her hand over his. They walked casually out of the bar, but as soon as they hit the sidewalk she broke into a run. He, still by the arm, was dragged along behind.

"What the fuck was that?" he said at a corner two or three streets up. He was working to catch his breath, which came in long labored plumes.

"That was fun," she said, and only then released his hand. He looked at her sideways.

"Yeah," he said, "I guess it was." They stood at the mouth of the Canal Street station.

"Thank you," she said, and there went his brow again—she could see he was about to ask her, For what? Well, that wasn't a question she was prepared to answer, so she threw her arms around him, the hug nearly over by the time he realized it was happening. She released him and was off running again: down the stairs, away. She sent a "good night" echoing up from around the corner of the landing where she'd disappeared.

Second date: Let's do something outside. They were in the midst of a warm spell, strange surprise in the dead of February, and he wanted to take advantage of what he called the "temporary reprieve." She was from New Hampshire and chalked the weird weather up to global warming—we're so fucked, she said; the whole world is—but anyway she agreed with him as far as getting some fresh air while they could.

They met in Long Island City, where the G and the 7 lines cross. (She lived in Sunnyside and he lived in Bushwick; they were fifteen minutes apart by car, but neither of them had one.) They walked down to the waterfront, where new high-rises were under construction. They snuck onto the private piers, then ended up on a baseball field in a nearby park, where she could feel him working up the nerve to kiss her, but they were interrupted by cops who drove right up onto the diamond with their lights on to inform them that city parks close at dusk. They went deeper into Queens, through a vaguely unsavory industrial area, past unfenced lots and over half-buried train tracks. The neighborhoods continued to shift until they found themselves on a small street with groomed trees complementing a bench. They sat down and had their first kiss, finally. She took him back to her apartment, to her room, and was astonished—though hardly unhappy—to find herself the target of his rampant, heaving need. Deep within her the pins in a lock were aligning; a book or a door was flung open.

When he excused himself to the bathroom she stayed supine, goggle-eyed in the low light of a desk lamp she kept on the floor at the room's far end, its neck craned back at the wall, casting a big bright spot like a shadow on fire.

In the morning they went to a Greek diner near her apartment and got breakfast specials. She mopped her syrup with her toast and said that places like this were the reason you lived in Queens. They saw each other again a few days later—she stayed over at his place—and before long it was almost every night: one apartment or the other, but mostly his. He liked to be in his own space, he said, and she was surprised to find herself acquiescing to him on this and other matters. He wasn't demanding or bossy; he just said what he wanted—that film looks insipid; I'd rather have Mexican—and assumed that if she disagreed with him she'd let it be known. That was reasonable for any couple, besides which she was no pushover. He'd learned that last semester, hadn't he? He seemed to have a clear vision of her in his head: a fickle piece of work whose attention he now commanded; a beautiful, wild girl whose heart he'd won. It made sense that he thought this; it was the bill of goods she'd sold him. She saw herself this way, too, sometimes, but in passing flashes: a phantom only ever glimpsed as it was slipping away. To herself she was the same insecure striver she had always been, who made a mantle of her outsider status not because she valued it so highly but rather because she could never figure out where the inside of anything was. There was a part of her that had never left middle school and never would. She knew this about herself and didn't like it. Her heart had an outer layer, steel tough but eggshell thin; beneath it she was all seething core.

He didn't care about music enough and had the worst taste in poetry. He read the silliest things imaginable—Stephen Dunn! It was impossible to respect his work, and she horrified herself with the lying reverences she produced by way of praise. He read her work with exacting patience and returned it scribbled blue with suggestions and line edits she had made a point of not asking for. They were three months in and had started to say "I love you." It was true.

Then one night in the fourth month he had a crying fit. They were in bed, lying close but apart, drowsing, when suddenly he sat up straight. Balled fists on the mattress and everything, like a little kid.

At first he was incoherent, not making words even, but eventually he got around to them, ranting for an hour, maybe longer, through and between choked sobs. What was he talking about? His argument—if that's what it was—had too many particulars and subpoints that entered the discourse, then dropped from it without notice or priority. The main gist, she gathered as he settled himself into timid sniffles, was that he was breaking up with her but hoped most earnestly that they might remain close as friends.

Her disbelief defied all analogy. She was cotton-mouthed and wide-eyed, had sat up at some point during his long aria, now fell flat backwards as if pushed (a feather'd have done the job nicely), and what should happen next but the schizoid snit slimed in for a presumptive farewell turn—wiped his face cursorily, incompletely, on a snatch of bedsheet and then was looming over her. So shocked was she that she kept still as he slid her panties kneeward. She regained herself and tucked those panty-bound knees up to her tits—she liked that word for them; he didn't and refused to say it, but no matter, they were dead to him now. She planted the rough flats of her feet against his soft furry chest and kicked him off her. He flailed and flew clear of the bed. She got dressed. He watched her from behind the bed, peering like a meerkat. How had she ever fallen into loving him? She stormed from the site of her shame into the deep city night.

He emailed her the next day. Remorse without retraction— the bastard truly wished to bury her in words, words, words. She blocked his address. Cal left her alone now, was even frightened of her or so it seemed and maybe he was right to be. He cut her wide berths in the hallways and at poetry readings. They didn't have class together, at least. Once she was riding in an elevator alone and he stepped onto it and the doors clunked shut before she could step out and he, oblivious in the depth of whatever was tinkling in his over-the-ear headphones, did not see her at first. By the time he did look up—she could feel his gaze snake across her body—she had smeared her own face over with a look that preemptively negated anything it might have occurred to him to say. She stared straight ahead into the gray brushed steel. The seconds ticked off and then the ride was finished. All told, they would not speak for a dozen years.

Abigail finished the MFA (as well Cal must have), then decided to go for a PhD. She studied abstruse, devastating theories and soon enough could drive them like knives through the soft guts of any TV commercial or radio hit—not that these great lumbering beasts of mass culture ever took note of their having been hunted and skinned. The work was not particularly easy, but neither was it overly challenging. It was interesting at first, and then it wasn't, but you got into a rhythm and then it was like anything you did for a living. Any job. And occasionally, when your pet theory, pushed to its intellectual asymptote, somehow turned inside out on you, you called this dialectics, turned the paper in anyway, let the long-haired guy from your German class take you out for a drink or two or five. He was Continental, indeed French, and looked like a true and total asshole with his neckerchief, but she knew the rules were different with Europeans and something about him whispered that he would not disappoint.

It turned out she was a genius for German. She was tutoring the poor Frenchman, who was merely bilingual—not that his English was any great shakes either. On her own time she rendered Hölderlin and Rilke into English with a felicity and art that her own work—the poetry or the crit stuff—rarely achieved.

Abigail cut the Frenchman loose when her orgasms became predictable. He gave them to her still but seemed to be doing it somehow lazily, which was not to be endured. Nearly two years passed without significant company. She took her degree. A university press took her thesis, a boring and sophisticated treatise that eight people would ever read. She was proud of it but also felt that it didn't matter. She took an assistant professorship at a private college in the Pacific Northwest and by her thirtieth birthday found herself in a position to think about buying a little house, which is just what she did.

She knew some men out West. One was an inveterate loser in perpetual self-consolation over a childhood episode of sexual abuse. He had stumpy blond dreadlocks, refused to give up on heavy metal, and had never held a job of any kind. She did not love him, but he wasn't as dumb as he might have been, and she appreciated his utter incompatibility with every aspect of her professional life. Also, there was his awful taste in music, which was the same as her awful own. That part she did love. He kept up regular correspondence with his molester, an old family friend with a position in state politics and a string of car dealerships up and down the coast. Dreadlocks drove a Lexus SUV, had been blackmailing the pervert lo these many years.

But the patron-criminal had carcinomas in uncertain remission and she knew Dreadlocks would lose his mind whenever the cancerous creep finally kicked, so she gave herself three months longer for indulgence's sake, then broke things unequivocally off. Dreadlocks plowed his SUV into a utility pole and was lucky to escape from the accident—if that's what it was—with nothing worse than two fractured ribs, a mild concussion, and a pile of fines from the city. These and his hospital bills were paid off by the molester, and likewise was the car replaced, though Dreadlocks's license was revoked for a year.

Who else did she date? A woman artist. A reticent priest. She finished many translations but did not publish them. It would be too easy and they'd garner her far too much acclaim. It was still her own verse that she loved. She sought a poetry press small, earnest, and middling enough that she might be its star.

And so Woodpile Editions, out of a suburbanized farmstead in Wichita. They ran an annual contest that cost ten dollars to enter. The prize was your book perfect-bound in an edition of five hundred, twenty-five of which were yours to keep, gratis, and you could buy as many more as you liked at the author discount (plus shipping). As soon as she'd seen the business card-size ad in the back of *Poets & Writers*, Abigail had known that she was home.

The publishers were a married pair of Berkeley refugees turned midwestern veterans; they drank wine out of teacups and had matching silver ponytails. Abigail's verse was gloomy and fitful and at first shocked them badly. Imagine her treasured Rilke at his highest-strung and the concerns of George

Garrett in "Buzzard"; crossbreed these, then refract the result through the operatic doom music to which she for some reason still gave equal credence. It was not bloodless, at least; her lines were stormy and kinked. Without question she was the most talented thing to have ever come their way, so they called her on the phone and told her she had won the contest. She volunteered to them that she meant to purchase the entire print run herself and in their instant and total thrill at this news they invited her out to Wichita to visit the home office and confer on the question of her cover art.

Abigail spent an excruciatingly charmed weekend on the plain, the result of which was the inevitable chiaroscuro calla lily set against a burnt umber field. The book's name and her own name would appear, respectively, above and below the lily in passable white serif. She gave a reading to an audience of seven, then went home. Two months later she received her shipment of the complete edition of her poetry—ten small boxes, fifty books in each one.

Her school gave her a reading, too, albeit grudgingly. The creative writing department did not like to see their action elbowed in on. But they knew what was politic, and there was even a reception afterward with crackers and three different cheeses, ice-cold soda cans and headache champagne. She drank more than she should have while a grad student volunteer sold her books for her. He was studying Chaucer as an antecedent of hip-hop and claimed to have read her book—not the one of poems, which he had only purchased that evening, but the theory one. She had ridden her bicycle to campus, as per usual, but was now quite drunk. He offered to drive her home. In her driveway he looked at her with his dark moist striving eyes and she told him to recline his seat back. She was thirty-four, but if you got her out of her professorial dress suit and into, say, jeans and a peasant blouse, she could still pass for twenty-seven. Naked you could see she was at least thirty, but her thirty made it seem like thirty was the great perfect age: a goal. Who needed those magazine teenagers hawking underwear and vodka? This woman looked like what it meant to be a woman, in her stunning adult prime. Not that the grad student was treated to such revelations. He never even saw her out of her coat. "Don't you make me regret this," she said in a flat, serious voice, leaning low over his lap and unzipping him, and he promised that he wouldn't, and he didn't, and so neither did she.

She wanted to go to the National Creative Writing Association Annual Literary Writing Conference and so appealed to her school for funds. Her request was denied. Her publishers agreed to split the cost of a table with her. She paid out of pocket for the flight and hotel. They sent a large stack of flyers announcing this year's incarnation of the contest; she herself was to be its honorable judge. She liked seeing her own name and thumbnail author photo on the top of the flyer. There was also a Woodpile banner, which she tacked to the front of the table.

The conference was in Denver that year. She sat for hours at her table, not selling any books at all. There were many seminars taking place in conference rooms, also panels and readings and lectures, all of which she skipped. In the evening she insinuated herself with some friendly strangers who claimed unanimous fealty to "avant-post-meta-narrative," though it was possible she'd gotten the prefix sequence wrong. They hailed from around the Southeast and ran some kind of website together. She followed them from one hotel bar cocktail hour to another, then retired to her own hotel for an On-Demand movie followed by a hot bath that lasted as long again.

The second day she put all the books she'd brought—a hundred of them, in a wheeled blue suitcase—out on the table in a careful pyramid. She made a sign that said PLEASE TAKE ONLY ONE. Beside these she put out the stack of flyers for the contest, and then she got up to walk around the fair, sneaking sidelong glances at university journals and small presses of every niche and distinction (or lack thereof). She was barely curious as to the natures of these outfits and sought mostly to protect herself from being shanghaied into chitchat, the inevitable segue to the sales pitch. This lack of interest, she recognized, was equally present in her would-be readership no less than in herself, and in this knowledge one could locate the precise central flaw of the entire enterprise. A cult of self-expression was throttling the life from the world.

Well, why not? All her favorite music of youth—which she still loved and believed in and blared constantly, both at home and in her office—heralded and celebrated apocalypse, devastation, chaos. She was nobody's savior and had no wish to be. Let the world save itself, if it could. She personally aspired to be part of the problem—to exacerbate the mess.

Abigail saw Cal sitting second from the end in a row of five men crammed cheek by jowl at a single table. CYGNUS LOOP COL-

LECTIVE, their banner read. Cal's face was grooved now and his hairline had hiked back a ways but sure as anything it was him. He was signing a book for somebody and did not see her. All around them young people rushed: boys with goatees and girls with bangs, everyone clutching official maps and shouldering tote bags misshapen with bulk. Maybe she was wrong about the conference-goers, the future of literature, and who knew what else. Or was it possible to be both wrong and right at once? Cal's customer walked away and he became focused on twirling his pen. Her shadow spilled over the white tablecloth and his books; he looked up.

They found a small sunny patch of grass outside the convention center and leaned with their backs against a giant decorative hunk of Colorado stone.

He'd worked construction at some point; his mother had died. He had left New York, returned, then left again. He was involved with the Unitarian church in his new hometown, which was conveniently just over on the other side of Boulder, though he'd been there four years, so was it really "new" anymore? (He actually asked her this—she shrugged.) He worked in sales for a regional brewery, did his books thing on the side. The year after they graduated, he said, he'd written the best poem of his life—the only good one he'd ever written, if the truth was to be told about it, and why shouldn't he tell the truth? He was content with his life now. He had long since figured out who he was. He looked at her meaningfully as he said this, as if his strange parenthetical glance could somehow hyperlink back through the years to both acknowledge and disown his behavior on that strange night that had ended their intimacy. So anyway he'd written the good poem and sent it to *Poetry* magazine—where it was accepted!—a victory that had nearly ruined him. There was a long struggle he mostly glossed over, the upshot of which was that he wrote prose now, considered himself a novelist. "But enough about me," he said.

She kept most of it to herself. He could always Google her. Perhaps he already had. She deflected their conversation back toward his life (it wasn't difficult) and in service of this aim feigned an interest in his "project," as he had called it with no hint of irony, no trace of shame.

"A sonnet in novels," he said.

"You mean a novel in verse?"

"No," he replied with a flash of the old maddening confidence. "Fuck John Wheelwright. I meant what I said."

It was to be a cycle of fourteen books, and their several titles taken together would form a sonnet—the very sonnet he'd had in *Poetry*, in fact. He expected to write one book every two years for twenty-eight years and complete the cycle in time for his sixty-fifth birthday. He'd finished and self-published Book One earlier this year and had brought it to Denver for its official debut. Cal, short for Calvert, was his middle name. "Cal" was the only thing anyone had ever called him, but as a published author he was F. Calvert Donovan. She felt sure she had known about the F. but couldn't remember whether she had ever known what it stood for. She did not ask about it now. Book One in his cycle was called *I Molt Backwards Through Time*, and though she couldn't help but notice that this phrase was four syllables too short for a sonnet line—to say nothing of the missing iambs—she chose not to spoil the moment and held her tongue.

Abigail could see that whatever had broken loose in Cal that hellish evening all those years ago had never been righted or healed. She felt special, in retrospect, to have witnessed the birth of such a deep and unyielding derangement. She said she would look his sonnet up. He said there was no need because it was printed as the frontispiece to the novel—and would be printed in each subsequent book as well, with the given titular line in boldface. She said she'd come by his table later, maybe tomorrow, and they could trade books.

A book of hers! Why hadn't she said anything sooner? But of course because what else would she be doing here? And a trade! It was too perfect! He'd be honored. What was it called?

"*Beloved Predator*," she said.

"It's so damn good to see you," he said, and reached over and gave her a hug. He was firmer now, more muscled in early middle age than he had ever been young. The construction work? The good mountain air? She was stiff in his arms at first but then leaned forward, pressed her chest against his and even got one arm around his shoulders—squeezed and counted three Mississippi before pulling back. He was slow in releasing her, then smoothed his shirt and said he had to get back to his table. He didn't know the Cygnus Loop guys too well—he'd met them through a listserv—and he didn't want to impose on their goodwill, but maybe they could meet up later that

evening at his "off-site" reading. This seemed to mean that
the event was not a part of the official conference program and
therefore not held on the convention center's grounds. He'd
secured the back room of a restaurant that unfortunately was
vegan, but the burritos were supposed to be decent, he said,
and anyway the drinks were cheap. He produced a small spiral
notebook like a reporter might carry, flipped it open to a blank
page, scribbled down the restaurant's name and address and
his own phone number, then ripped the page out and folded
it in half. On the outside of the fold he wrote in spindly block
capital letters the title of his novel, then underlined it: _I MOLT
BACKWARDS THROUGH TIME_. "So you don't forget what
it's for," he said. "I know how hectic the conference gets." He
pressed the folded paper into her palm with both hands. They
stood; he hugged her again, then turned and jogged, nearly
sprinted, back inside. She lingered in the grass, watching the
long glass faces of the downtown buildings flash fire-gold in
the sinking western sun.

Back at her table she saw that all the flyers for the contest
had been taken, and her sign knocked over, but her pyramid
of books had not been so much as jostled. Her monument was
perfectly undisturbed. She did not know whether to feel in-
jured or pleased. All those copies of her precious book—she
left them as they were. Let the janitors puzzle over them or
slide them unread into a black vat of trash. It no longer mat-
tered, if it ever had, and there were four hundred more copies
boxed up unvanquished back at her Oregon home. Her work
would become a little more rare, was all, which maybe wasn't

such a bad thing. The torn-off page with Cal's phone number on it seemed to warm the pocket in which it lay. She was a beautiful woman in a smart dress and dark stockings. The world itself seemed to barely know what to do with her. She had no old friends.

CAROL, ALONE

Seventy-two years old and I'm the last person I know who drinks real coffee. Everyone else gave in to decaf years ago. Bad hearts, they've got, or they don't want to be kept up. Gerald felt that coffee was the root cause of my insomnia but I never could believe that and I still don't. A strong cup in the morning hardly keeps me from a nap in the afternoon. It is only in the night I lie awake, alert and tossing, denied entry to the vault of sleep. Sometimes, when I know in my bones there will be no rest no matter what, I get out of bed and go make myself a cup and drink it while I watch TV or pace the house or sit out on the back porch and listen to the night: crickets and groaning air conditioners and faraway cars.

Tonight I've found a documentary about the ruins of São Paulo Cathedral in Macau. Built by Jesuits in the 1500s, operated for three hundred years or so, burnt down in 1835. Why never rebuilt? The program doesn't say. But the stone facade survived the fire and has stood freely ever since. There's a long shot of it silhouetted in sunset light, then a station break. All the commercials are for tax attorneys and prescription drugs. A fat-faced man in a blue suit says, "Bankruptcy isn't the end— it's a new beginning!" Grinning AARP members in tracksuits chat about pills for their bladders, memory, blood sugar, skin, pain, sleep—everything managed and nothing solved, ask your doctor today.

When the program returns there are close-ups of the church's stonework. The camera lingers over waggle-tongued demons, gray saints, a great ship frozen among scrolling waves. I imagine climbing the steep steps, can practically feel the is-land sun on our necks and arms and Gerald's bald spot (he preferred visors to hats), pausing to catch our breath and mop our brows in the relative comfort of the facade's shadow before passing through its tall archway and into the hot open land that was once the cathedral. "By now it's been nothing for almost as long as it was ever something," I say, speaking the words aloud to the empty living room. The program says that the grounds have been made a World Heritage Site. And so the ruin's future is secure, its preservation assured.

The program ends but the night keeps going.

Thirty-five years apiece in the New York City public school system—I taught high school English; Gerald taught middle school science and a bit of shop. Twenty-nine of those thirty-five years in the row house in the Slope, riding the subway and raising the boys and hacking away at the mortgage and finally owning it outright just in time to sell when we took our retirements and went south—before the market did, thank God. "Turncoat," my sister, Elsie, said about us leaving. "You've gone soft." But Elsie and Donald never had children—they couldn't—so what would she know about it?

We moved to a development called Canyon Lakes. This being South Florida, there is of course no canyon. As for the so-called lakes, they are skinny man-made channels of murky water in which you can neither fish nor swim. They ribbon through the development, brushing property lines so that every unit can be listed as "waterfront." We do get birds, ducks and heron, sometimes ibis, and minnows at the grass banks for visiting grandkids to catch in Dixie cups and torture—they squeeze them between their fingers and the little fish burst like grapes.

My son Dennis is still in the city, but Keith, the older one, came down about a year after we did, for a job that ended up falling through—but he found something else and stayed. He met Heather and married her and they live twenty minutes down the road in a development like ours, only it's townhouses instead of stand-alones and the people there are younger: buying their first homes, starting their families. We have a clubhouse with a little theater; they have a community center with a little playroom. Everything in its right place, I suppose, though that does beg the question of what Keith and Heather are doing there. "We're waiting for the right time," Keith always says, and then refuses to elaborate at all. I have dinner with my son and his wife once a week.

We had six, nearly seven good years in Florida, despite the onset of what Gerald called "old folks' disease"—his catchall for the host of complaints and small agonies that infringe with the gaining years. Our joints ached; we were advised to watch how we ate. We caught fewer colds in the warm weather, yes, but whatever we caught would linger. Gunked sinuses. Aspirin regimens. Prescription bottles in the medicine cabinet, on the nightstand, by the kitchen sink—chatting about side effects like the people on TV. We got good about sunscreen. We stood on the decks of cruise ships. Then Gerald got sick in his lungs and then he died.

All our New York years I kept my hair short—very sensible and teacherly, and only ever dyed its own natural color. In Florida I found all the ladies wore their hair like this, permed or close-cropped or whatever it took to mask the thinning and recession, keep themselves regulars at the salon, give themselves somewhere to go. I had no intention of living like that, besides which my hair is still nearly as thick as when I was a girl, so as soon as we got here I stopped coloring it and grew myself a white braid that was all the talk of the clubhouse whenever I went in for a turn on the StairMaster or a dip in the pool.

The night I left Gerald's body at the hospital I came home and cut my braid off, coiled the limp thing up like a length of rope, stuck it in a jewelry box, and shut the lid. Now I'm one more short-haired widow after whom nobody whispers. Sometimes while I'm exercising I'll wonder, What is the point of this? The hope is for health, of course, and that the sunlight and heat and exertion will prove exhausting, set the foundation for a good night's well-earned rest. Sometimes it happens this way, but not often. It's more like my body and mind are disconnected, my days and nights non sequitur to each other. Sometimes I feel like the hole in my life is even larger than my life ever was and that I live inside it, potted like a houseplant in the soil of my grief.

Midmorning I make a pot of coffee and set it out on the counter to cool. I put the TV on but there's nothing good to watch: soap operas on the networks, shouting anchors on the cable news, and either way you get more commercials for lawyers and drugs. I shut the TV off, put a load of laundry in, then go outside.

By day my patio with its peach-colored tiles hardly seems to be the same place I pass my endless nights. I sit down at the table—tempered glass on a white metal frame; the chairs woven plastic, also white; and all of it lightly filmed in dirt—and am staring out through my fine-mesh black bug screens at the houses across the calm brown water when, with a kind of calm shock, I notice something so utterly unexpected it hardly occurs to me to be afraid. An alligator—gray-green, perhaps seven feet nose to tail, having apparently crawled out of the water and up the stumpy step of the low bank—has laid itself out in a sunny spot halfway up my grass and fallen asleep.

Leaves rustle in the breeze. The sun is high.

I know I ought to call someone, an authority, the authorities—police or animal control or 311. I can dial the gatehouse. Charles, or Guillermo or Rose, whoever is on duty, will know what to do. This development, this whole county,

was swampland not so long ago. It's not so crazy that a dis-
placed creature would wander home again. This can't be the
first time it's happened. There surely must be procedures in
place. But he feels like my secret, even though he's right out
there in the open where anyone can see him and, for all I know,
has. Perhaps some other, more prudent citizen has done the
needful thing and made the call, is on the phone this very
instant with a man in a county uniform who is saying, "Could
y'all repeat that, please?" as though Mrs. Markowitz or whoever it chances to be were a crowd unto herself. But somehow
I don't think that's happening. He is a beautiful animal and I
think that he is mine.

In the house the phone is ringing. Not without reluctance, I
get up and go into the living room, to the end table next to the
couch. I check the name on the caller ID and my heart sinks:
Ed Roman. Ed is a neighborhood man whose memory is shot.
His wife, my friend Marlene, talks incessantly of the need to put
him in a home, how she can't bear to do such a thing, and the
peace she will know when it is finally done.

"Hello," I say, twisting and untwisting the curled phone
cord as I squint across the living room, through the sliding
glass door and past the patio, but the yard slopes in such a way
that from where I'm standing the sleeping creature has fallen
out of view.

"Hello, Carol," Ed says. "How are you? Everything's well?"

"Wonderful. I'm just finishing up the breakfast dishes.
Would you like to talk to Gerald?"

"If you please."

"Well, I'm afraid he's out right now, Ed. A gator crawled out of the lake today and he chased it off with my broom. Foolhardy, I know, but that's Gerald."

"My God."

"Then it was straight to the hardware store to price fencing."

"Oh boy," Ed says. "Now that's a job."

"What can I say, Ed? Gerald loves a project. I'll tell him you called."

"Thank you, dear."

I hang up the phone and rush back outside, knowing with perfect certainty that the animal will be gone and then seeing that he is gone without a trace, no ripples in the water, no flat spot in the grass. I go back inside and get a rag and the 409 and go back out and wipe down the table and the chairs. I go back in and check the coffee and, finding it room temperature, serve myself some over ice in a clear glass mug and pour cream into it and watch as the cream seeps and trickles around the ice cubes and against the glass, the dark drink blurring pale. I take it back outside and sit down at my now clean table to wait, but nothing comes. Well, not nothing. There are blue jays and dragonflies; a gardener across the lake prunes back a flowering bush whose branches have grown across a doorway. An escaped house cat stalks a squirrel he'll never catch—there's a small brass bell hung from his collar—passing through the very space where the alligator slept.

The den is a beige room—they're all beige rooms—with a big window and warm tiles because I never draw the shade. Gerald called the den the computer room because we keep our PC there. Keith set it up for us and whenever he's over he'll fuss with it—update programs, move folders around, whatever he does. Gerald used to pay close attention to these ministrations but he never seemed to understand what he saw. Me, I can check my email and otherwise prefer to ignore the computer altogether, but my sister, my God, she fills out these surveys. She finds these websites where you sign up and do them and then they send you coupons and gift cards. Elsie will fill out any survey if she wants what the reward is and if she doesn't fit the criteria for respondents she lies. "If I didn't I would never get to do any," she says. "Nobody cares what an old woman thinks, but I make sure they know."

So the in-box: There's a summary of my accumulated points on a certain credit card, and three forwards from my brother-in-law, who has become a one-man distribution center for hoary old brain teasers, animated pictures of animals, political op-eds falsely attributed to celebrities, and racist knock-knock jokes. I don't know where in creation he comes by such stuff, much less why he passes it along to me and the dozen or so other people on his email list. He never asks me if I've read these things or what I thought of them. For him, the payoff seems to be in the act of forwarding itself. I believe it makes him feel like a player in the modern world.

Marlene calls, beside herself: "You won't believe what Ed said to me. I can't even tell you, I shouldn't, I'm sorry, but this is too much."

"Honey," I say to her. "You just let it all out." As I listen to her talking and crying, I keep doing this thing where I wrap the phone cord tight around my fingers until it hurts, then count to five and let the cord go. The pads of my fingers blanch white and then flush pink again; it's like watching the tide.

I have dinner with Keith and Heather. Their development is called Vista Trace. Tonight they've brought in takeout from a rotisserie chicken place that they call "the chicken place," which is close enough to its real name that I wonder why they don't just say the right thing. My daughter-in-law stabs at her steamed broccoli with a fork that already holds a wet flag of chicken skin draped over a corkscrew of mac and cheese. I break up an oily cornbread biscuit with my fingers, steal a glance at the clock.

In the old days I was never alone. When Elsie and I were girls we lived in Borough Park with lots of family nearby: cousins on every corner, or so it seemed. Our aunt Bessie had a candy store on Avenue J and Coney Island Avenue. That place! Like a dream now—only I'm not dreaming. I'm awake and wandering aimlessly in the old halls of my head. The candy store had a marble counter and a soda fountain and a big display of magazines and newspapers. We went there after school for a float or a sundae and for Bessie to watch us until Mom got off work. She worked in the office of a pocketbook factory and our father was a butcher. He'd been a garment salesman before the Depression, but when things got bad his father-in-law, my grandpa Izzy, said, "If you're a butcher you'll always eat, at least." Izzy had been through hard times in Poland. So my father learned butchering and he was good right from the start but he hated it. He worked at a storefront on Union Street and after the War, when things turned around, he always talked about quitting but he never did. Maybe once he could have been something else, but the Depression had made him a butcher. We didn't know all this as girls of course: who was struggling, what the reasons were, what they'd given up or lost. Everything seemed normal to us because it was all we knew, like Bessie's husband, Morris, sitting in the back of the candy store, reading Torah—I used to know the Yiddish word for it, what they called the men who read Torah all day—and never helping with the store at all. She married him late and he worked her like a horse. Bessie did the books, she placed the orders, stood out front, everything, and probably the only reason she had taken him was to have kids—I mean it must have been—but either they couldn't or he wouldn't because they never did. Really Bessie was my great-aunt, Grandpa Izzy's sister; they'd come over together in the 1890s, when she was about the same age as Elsie and I were when we used to go and sit at her shop. Such a strain on that woman! And on top of everything else being responsible for the two of us sitting at the marble counter, our school friends, too, swiveling our red stools so we spun in circles and crying if any soda should spill on our dresses. Bessie must have known by that time we were the closest she was going to get to girls of her own. After she died Morris sold the candy store, and so it passed out of our family and a few years after that it closed down. And to think that I'm older now than any of them were then—except maybe for Izzy, who left Poland not knowing his own birthday or exactly what year he'd been born. He always said, How can I worry about my age when I don't even know it?

I'm woken by the phone, on the couch, having fallen asleep—finally—during *Good Morning America*. I see on the caller ID that it's Dennis, my younger son. I let the machine get it. He says, "Mira fell off the jungle gym at recess and broke her arm. Everything's okay, we took both girls out of school, and we're all at the hospital; she's being a trouper and I thought you'd appreciate—anyhow we'll send pictures of the cast after her friends all sign it." The machine clicks off.

I wait ten minutes before calling him back. I tell him I just got in from running some errands. He puts Mira on and I tell her to be a good girl and brave. Then Rebecca comes on and I tell her to be brave, too, and take good care of her sister. Then, since I've talked to everybody else, Dennis's wife comes on to say hello. I ask her how she's holding up. "Pretty good, all things considered." A pause on her end, then, "How are you, Carol?"

"I don't sleep," I say. "I don't sleep and I hate this god-damned being alone." Instantly I am abashed, thinking that perhaps the worst part of grief is how it inexorably pivots any and every thing back toward itself. It has made me pitiful and selfish and I hate it, and so on top of everything else it has made me hateful, too.

I force myself to break the silence on the line. "Jessica, I'm sorry. This wasn't the time and I didn't mean— Everything is fine here. I'm well."

"It's okay," she says. "I wouldn't have asked if I didn't want to know. But listen, Carol, it's important to me for you to know that you are not alone. We're all right here with you." I can picture her standing in a green hospital corridor, wearing a charcoal business suit and a thin gold necklace, my son's cell phone in one hand and the other hand cupped over her other ear, her wedding ring flashing when it catches the light. It occurs to me that her well-meant words are both true and not true.

At my checkup Dr. Greene asks after my sleep schedule. He suggests—not for the first time—that I let him prescribe a sleeping pill. I always refuse because they seem like a crutch, or like they could become one. "But the purpose of a crutch," Dr. Greene says, "is to relieve pressure. So the thing that's been broken can heal." I don't say anything to him. He smiles, puts a hand on my shoulder and squeezes. "You'll try it and you'll see," he says.

The first night I take the pill sleep comes swift as rain and I am grateful despite turbulent dreams. The second night is even better: oblivion, pure and sweet. But the third night sleep will not come, even after I take a second dose, so I lie flat on my back in my bed while the pills murmur through me, amorphus shapes flickering rosy and golden in the deep of the bedroom sky.

When the sun rises I put on a pot of coffee, toss the orange canister in the trash.

Marlene comes over early for our outing: to the cemetery to see Gerald, to the nursing home to see Ed, and then an early dinner either at the TooJay's next to the mall or the Cheesecake Factory in it. Normally when we go out together we fuss awhile first over who will drive—each of us insisting that the other need not trouble herself—but today I'm only too eager to seize on her lame excuse of having blocked me in.

We don't stay long at the cemetery. When Gerald first died I used to talk when I came here, bring him up to speed about our children and friends, the neighborhood—anything I could think of. But whatever this was supposed to make me feel, it didn't, besides which I hated doing it. If Gerald is anywhere he can hear me, I figure, then he probably already knows what little news I have to bring. Another of our old friends kicks off, he's bound to see them before I can get here to see him. And if he's not anywhere, which is, after all, what we both always expected would be the case, then what am I doing recapping TV shows and mah-jongg winnings to a patch of earth? So I come and stand around for a few minutes with my head down, place a rock on the headstone; then Marlene and I go pay respects to a few other people we know who are buried here, but she has some trouble with her knees and in the sun it's pushing ninety, so before we know it we're back in her Cadillac. "My boat," she says, grinning reflexively at her favorite of her own few jokes. "One of these days I'll pick a name for it, get it painted on the trunk."

"Big white letters," I say.

"Fancy cursive script," she adds.

"But what do you call it?"

"*The Part D.*"

Laughing, we pull into the parking lot of the nursing home where Ed now lives. The building is painted the same peach color as my patio.

Ed seems smaller, like some animal that fits itself to whatever shell it finds. He likes that they let him wear his pajama clothes all day long instead of making him get dressed, like Marlene always used to, even though they had nowhere to go.

"How's Gerald?" he asks me.

"Ed, you know better," Marlene says, exasperated, even as I say, "Oh, he says hello."

Marlene and I look at each other. I look away, down, at Ed, who says nothing, the paradox of our answers either somehow resolved or else unregistered in his mind. I excuse myself to the restroom and don't come back. I take a seat in the lobby and then text Marlene that I will wait for her there. I pick up a magazine from a table and flip the pages without looking at them. It occurs to me I have no idea how long this visit is supposed to last. Is the fact that Ed will probably forget we were ever here an argument for staying as long as possible, or does it excuse cutting things short? How much time is enough time?

"I'm sorry," I say to Marlene. We're standing in the parking lot; she's fishing in her purse for her keys. "I know I shouldn't have done that, but it seemed . . . kinder."

"Pity isn't kindness," Marlene says, and I don't say that Ed was hardly the one I was trying to be kind to. "It's important to get him to focus—to retain things. Even if he can't do it he must try. It's the only way to, the only way to keep him here." I walk around the car and hug Marlene, whose whole body is shudder-ing. Her skin feels like a piece of paper that has gone through the laundry folded up in a pocket. Gently, I pull her keys from her hand; she lets me have them. Her rings are so loose on her fingers it's hard not to take them, too.

Marlene says I should go to my house and she's fine to get herself home from there, but I won't have it. I drive her back to her house, cut the engine, and apologize again. She tells me to please just forget it, unbuckles her safety belt, opens the passenger door. I give her her keys back and she says we'll make dinner up—later this week or next, some night there's no mah-jongg, we'll figure it out. We say our good-byes and I set out to walk across the development back to my house. I cross a street. I see a crow. It is evening, the sky orange-pink at its rim and blue as winter up above. A few jet trails and a pale scrim of moon. I walk past palms and bougainvillea, dec-orative grapefruit trees and spiky ferns. Lizards skitter across the sidewalk, its curve tracing the shape of the fake lake as it leads me home.

It's late when I hear the noise outside. I mute the TV, put my slippers on and pass through the dark house and slide the glass door open and step onto the patio. Through the bug screens the house lights on the far side of the water seem to twinkle like distant stars. I can see a shape among the shadows; something out there is alive.

I hit the perimeter lights. A couple of teenagers appear in my grass. The girl is on top of the boy, her hair in a tight braid past her shoulders, blue veins glowing beneath the pale skin of her chest. Her shirt in the grass beside them; his jeans are open but not pushed down. She jumps to her feet but then stands there, making no attempt to cover herself, squinting her eyes toward the patio as if she can't quite see me through the suddenly glaring light.

"This was very stupid," I say, in my most imposing teacher voice, only slightly betrayed now by a quaver as I get louder. "Monumentally stupid. It's dangerous out here at night—you have no idea!"

"Lady, this is like the most boring place on earth," the boy says, rising to his feet with the girl's shirt in his hand, positioning himself behind her as though he were the one half undressed. She reaches back for the shirt and takes it, brings it forward and holds it up in both hands, shakes a few blades of grass from the fabric and only then grudgingly puts it on before walking off without so much as a word. The boy follows close on her heels through the succession of unfenced yards. When I'm sure they're gone I shut the lights off and go back in.

In the fridge there are two boneless chicken breasts, a pound of lean ground beef I'd meant for meatballs, and a packet of deli-sliced turkey. I gather it all into my arms and carry it out to the patio, out the screen door, into the dark. I kneel in the warm grass and peel back wrappers—the first chicken breast bounces off a tree trunk; the second hits the water with a plop. I toss the slick deli rounds like Frisbees and they land like lily pads but sink after a few seconds. Cold beef squishes between my fingers and mucks up under my nails. I ignore the rising drone of flies that my work has drawn, focusing instead on a welcome wave of exhaustion coming over me, and what a blessing it would be to ride that wave—lie down in the grass by the calm black water, wake up next to my husband on a white beach in Macau.

SAINT WADE

We lived in a sludge-colored building with open-air hallways and stairs. My unit was on the second floor and faced the road. Terese and Mazie had a ground-floor unit that faced the back lot and a shuttered strip mall across the way. (You couldn't call them apartments, quite, but "rooms" seemed sad, somehow, so I went with units. The building itself I called the Hardluck Arms.) I was in my unit, watching a nature program about sharks. It said that because of how their gills work, sharks can never stop swimming or they drown. Now what would that be like, I wondered, to live your whole life in motion—to never even know what it meant to rest?

This was in Alabama in a small town I think it's fair to assume you've never heard of, halfway between Tuscaloosa and Mobile. The closest decent-size place is actually Meridian, but I was having a disinclination toward Mississippi around that time. My little brother, Benny, was a lawyer in Tallahassee, which was—in the other direction—far but not as far as it felt like; Florida can be that way. And he had a beach house on the panhandle in Carrabelle, which was even closer: six hours, about, and you could do it in less if you took 43 to 10 and didn't stop to eat. I hadn't had occasion—that is, invitation—to visit Benny in a while, but when I did go I preferred the smaller roads and the slower pace. If you were of a certain mind-set, say my ex-wife's, you might read quite a bit into that statement. But then if you were my ex-wife you might do all kinds of things, such as the things you did (or I thought you did) that made me do what I did—no reason to rehash particulars here—the upshot of all of which is her back with her mother in Oxford, and me disinclined toward Mississippi, established here at the Hardluck Arms.

Mazie was Terese's daughter, age three, blessed gift of a marital—if it was marital—disaster which I understood to have been similar enough to what I'd gone through to sympathize fully and not ask too many questions. Nobody ever gets free of the past, of course, but there's something to be said for living as though you could or even already have. If not you might just crawl into your own backstory like a cave and sit there on your rented bed, brooding to death in the Hardluck dark.

Anyway I first met the girls in the laundry room. I was walking out with my things and had to squeeze past them because Terese had her heaping basket on her knee, barely keeping it steady with one hand, and meanwhile her kid's longways under her other arm, wriggling and squirming and shrieking with pain-in-the-ass delight. I put my things down on a dryer.

"Hey, you need a hand," I said. It wasn't a question. "Pick one for me to hold while you get the other settled." Thought I was being cute but then she handed me the kid. I cooed and bounced her while Terese put the wash in. She packed it so tight I wondered if the clothes could even move around in there, and if the machine would handle the weight without straining to break, but I got that she didn't want to pay for two machines. Every penny, right?

Terese was wearing these jeans shorts that cupped her rear, a damn nice one, I thought, for a mother or otherwise. Blue plastic flip-flops and sunglasses, toenails freshly painted seasick green—I liked it. She got her detergent poured and turned to face me, the machine groaning to life behind her. She had gray eyes and was maybe five years older than I'd took her for when I was looking at her ass.

She was a waitress at the P. F. Chang's over in Thomasville and worked the dinner shift, so getting her out on a date was tough. We always got a late start and then there was the extra time to pay the babysitter for. She had this high school girl she used. I offered—gallantly, I thought—to cover the sitter from whenever she met up with me until whenever we got back to the Arms. At first that came to just a couple hours, but one night she came back to my unit for a nightcap and things got interesting and then we kind of nodded off and woke up and it was three a.m., her cell ringing—the poor sitter in tears. Had we had an accident? What was her own father going to think when she dragged home at such an hour? She hardly seemed relieved to learn that we were right upstairs.

So we hatched a new plan. I would babysit while Terese was at work, and she would bring back a doggie bag for us to have a late dinner with when she got home, by which time Mazie would hopefully be asleep and we could have our late-night date right there in her unit. We would try it and see. Which gets me back to where I left off when I started telling it: I was watching my shark show.

When it ended I shut off the TV, cranked the window open, and sat in my chair chain-smoking so I'd be good and nic'd up and not want one too bad while I was with the kid. Terese hadn't ever said that I couldn't (or that I could) smoke in front of Mazie, but I had noticed that she herself usually tried to hide it, and anyway the general gist these days seems to be that kids aren't supposed to see.

I stubbed my butt, closed the window, striped some Old Spice on my jeans to cover up any leftover smoke smell, hustled downstairs, and was right on time.

Mazie was on the floor in front of the couch, watching a video. Cartoon sunflowers were singing a song about needing rain and sunshine both to grow up tall. Everything in its right place; there is a season; all good things in all good time. I couldn't help but wonder, Is it healthy that we sell kids this load of horseshit and then they have to find out how it really is the hard way later on? I for one did not feel any taller for having been rained on. On the other hand, what you would say if you told them the truth wasn't anything you'd want to put in the mouth of a flower and set to a tune.

"Are you ready to cooperate with Wade?" Terese asked her daughter.

"I coperate!" Mazie said without turning from the TV.

"Good girl," her mother said. Then, to me, "Christ, I'm late. Okay, well, you two have fun."

I walked Terese to her own front door and held it open for her. She put her arms round my neck for a hug. I put my arms around her waist, grazing her hips with my hands as I went by, then giving her a good squeeze when I had her wrapped up. She squeezed me back and her face was in my neck hollow and she laid a quick kiss there as tight heat prickled up my spine. I was feeling very focused all of a sudden, or somehow more awake than I had been a moment ago—something important, I understood dimly, was about to change or perhaps already had. We let each other go and I cleared my throat. She went out the door and I shut it behind her. The sound drew Mazie's attention. "Mommy?" she said and, not seeing her, started to wail.

She let me pick her up and so I rocked her until she fell asleep in my arms; then I put her in her crib, which was right there in a corner of the living room. Terese's unit was bigger than mine, but that only meant it was two rooms instead of one.

When Mazie woke up again she was more like the happy kid I knew. She didn't seem to miss her mom at all. I took her out of her crib. We played peekaboo and colored pictures on paper towels, then hung them up on the fridge with magnets like our own little gallery show. I put the radio on and danced with her and even sang, which is not something I do at the drop of a hat. We were blasting the classic rock station. I even did the high parts on "Reelin' in the Years." When she was tired again I put her back down in her crib. When Terese unlocked the front door and peeked her head in, the very first thing I said to her was "Shhh."

I started spending most evenings a week with Mazie—some days, too, Terese now taking all the shifts she could get—and most nights I stayed over in their unit and when Terese had a day off we might all take a walk or go shopping. We knew what we looked like and we didn't mind. And when I was alone with Mazie it was the same: We ate peanut butter and banana sandwiches. We watched the singing sunflowers till I knew their songs by heart, as good as I ever knew "Reelin'" or "Stairway" or "Help." I made omelettes for both my girls for breakfast, drove Mazie to the park and chased her around. She got fresh air and exercise and we pet people's dogs there and I pushed her on the swing. I only ever told her to call me Wade. In fact, I didn't know whether the word "Daddy" was even in her vocabulary until the day she looked up from her coloring and called me it. She wanted me to hand her the blue crayon and she had to ask me twice before it registered who she was talking to, and a third time before I managed to do it.

Later that night I mentioned to Terese what had happened.

"That's swell," she said.

"And yet you don't seem overjoyed," I said.

"I'm glad you two get along, Wade."

"You make it sound like we're poker buddies."

"Listen," she said. "I'm only saying one thing, and the one

thing I'm saying is goddamnit, don't you build up all the heart that little girl has, then go and break it."

I told her I heard her loud and clear. It was well understood. I knew right where she was coming from.

"You're saying all the right things," she said, "and that's good. But it's not the talking that counts, and we both know it. You go ahead and remember what I said."

I helped a guy I knew out with a job he was doing—moving furniture, basically, but I don't want to get into the boring details— and I dedicated a portion of the proceeds from that venture to a night out for me and Terese, just us: a proper date. When we got home Mazie was sleeping and the sitter was watching the TV. Some movie stars were panting against the side of a brick building. The man held a silver pistol and was bleeding from his forehead. "It looks bad," the woman said sorrowfully, then instead of trying to stop the bleeding leaned in and kissed the man. When she pulled her face away it was bloody, too. I think the sitter wished we'd stayed out longer, but she took my money and left. Terese was in the bathroom, and I began to think about what I meant to say to her because it felt like the time had come to say something and I wanted it to be the right thing. I liked Terese, we were doing well together, and what we had was very agreeable, comfortable, beneficial to all parties, and a good time besides. So how do you say that to a woman? You don't, I guess, and sometimes when a woman says she loves you and you are inside of her there is nothing for it but to say so back and wish to Christ to make it true.

I packed my few belongings up and moved them to the unit downstairs.

It was after seven but the sun was still high. Terese was fresh off a day shift. She'd changed out of her uniform into a robe and meant to take a shower, but was so far lying cross the couch, feet up, Mazie on her stomach.

"What'd you and Wade do today, honey?"

"I go swings."

"Again?" Terese said. I wasn't sure if she meant that as a question to Mazie or to me.

"She loves the swings," I said. "And the slide, too. Didn't we slide today, Mazie?"

There was a box of mac and cheese in the pantry, but we'd made a box the night before, and Mazie'd had the leftovers for lunch.

"Listen," I said, "how starving are you? We need some things anyhow. I could make a quick Publix run, bring back a rotisserie chicken."

"Pick it up last thing before you get in line," Terese said, "and it should still be hot when you get home."

"Aye, aye, captain," I said.

"Aye, capan!" Mazie said.

"I can bring her with me if you want," I said. "Take your shower in peace."

"I haven't seen my kid all day," she said. I felt guilty. Here she had been out working while we had fun. Well, that was the arrangement, but still. Then Terese surprised me. She picked

Mazie up off her belly and held her in the air. "You know what," she said, "a long shower sounds like heaven. So go on—all yours."

We made our way up and down the aisles, Mazie in the kid seat, goggling at all the colorful boxes and lights, babbling away. Peanut butter, white bread, strawberry ice cream, cans of soup. The cartons of cigarettes are locked up at the front so you ask when you get to the register. Fish sticks, more mac and cheese boxes because you can pretty much never have enough. Bunch of bananas. Can of Maxwell House. There were vitamins in the medicine aisle. I passed them by, but the notion stuck in my mind. I was over in prepared foods, deciding if I wanted to bring home a half pound of potato salad to go with the chicken or if greens of some kind would be better. I stuck a pin in this question and circled back around to the pills. There were the Flintstones ones and the "Compare to" ones. They were exactly the same. Everyone knows that. If I put the boxes side by side and read the fine print I would even know for sure. They were probably made at the same factory. There was probably some website you could go to and read all about it.

Aw hell, I thought, *just this once*. And bought the good ones.

"You're a real saint sometimes, Wade," Terese said when I showed her what I'd got. "Do you know that?" I laughed at this and she laughed with me and kissed me and I imagined myself in my saintly robes and haloed, Saint Wade, patron of wildlife shows and the cigarette tax, bestower of name-brand vitamins, who shall rise up in glory and see that the waitresses of the Lord clock in at the pan-Asian bistro on time.

But some things are out of anybody's power, even saints'. Terese's job turned bad overnight, the way these kinds of jobs will. She got passed over for shift manager, was the first thing, and then corporate decided that everyone had to push a new special, which was this lemongrass seafood dish. They put all the girls on a quota for specials sold per night. This went against what you might call Terese's style. She was not going to push folks toward a nineteen-dollar plate of rice with a few shrimp and squid pieces thrown on top—one, because she thought it was stupid, and two, because when the customers were pissed at the end of their dinner it'd be her tip they took it out on. So her numbers suffered and she'd get bawled out and then come home and start bawling me out about whatever she could think up, and at first I was just taking it, but of course a man can only take so much, and we knew each other well enough by now to be cruel and soon it became a kind of nightly ritual to split a twelve-pack and tear each other apart. I never hit her, for whatever that's worth, but it was a hell of a place for a kid. Some nights I didn't sleep at all and ended up sitting on the couch in the dark, concentrating on the sound of Mazie's breathing, barely audible over the wheeze of the old window unit. Just sitting there, listening and drinking, trying not to think and thinking anyway. *Shark*, I thought.

The days after those nights always felt like they were over before they started. All I wanted was to get Terese off to work, pop the flower video in for Mazie, and try to catch up on some of the sleep I'd missed. I'd nap on the couch with my face turned away from the TV, barely dozing, still at the ready in case Mazie needed me, and consequently any dreams I managed to have were warped by the singing sunflowers in their endless encore medley of greatest hits.

One day I had had enough. I couldn't take another round of the same old songs or any of it. After we said good-bye to Terese I got Mazie dressed and put some Goldfish crackers in a baggie for her for later. I set her car seat up in my car and we hit the road.

We drove the smallest roads I knew of, out into the Florida-looking part of Alabama, where the sun flashes like a searchlight through stands of oak and tall pine thick with Spanish moss. We were headed for the Port of Mobile, where when me and Benny were little our father used to take us to sit and watch the boxcars load onto the boats. We'd loved it like nothing else. I was going to take Mazie there and we were going to take a picture on my phone of us waving and I was going to send it to Benny, and he'd call and want to know who she was and I'd tell him, and he'd mention the next time he was going to be down in Carrabelle, and I'd suggest that maybe we could meet him there, spend the weekend, and he'd say, Yeah, man, sure thing, love to have you, brother. And that would be the beginning of our new start—me and Terese's, Benny's and mine. I didn't see any reason Mazie wouldn't like the port as much as me and Benny had. There were stevedores in yellow hard hats and huge, graceful, slow-moving cranes that hoisted the freight through the air. But my favorite were the boats with railroad tracks built right into their decks so that the train cars could roll right up onto them. I bet she'd never seen a thing like that before. Those boats sailed out into Mobile Bay, then across the Gulf, and made ports of call in Mexico, where the cars rolled right off onto Mexican tracks, ready to go wherever they were going.

And who knows, maybe they still do, but it turns out you can't go to the Port of Mobile and watch the docks anymore. Some terrorism protocol, the guard at the gate said, and when he turned us away I found that I didn't have it in me to get worked up over one more way in which I had either been fucked over or come up short. Mazie and me split fries and a chocolate Frosty—I took a picture of her with chocolate all over her face and sent it to Terese, who didn't respond, though come to think of it she probably wasn't allowed to keep her phone on her when she was working, so I guessed she'd see it when she could and hopefully think it was cute and not lace into me later for fattening up her kid.

We got back on the road and were cruising up this two-lane highway, out in the country again, going fast but also taking our time. There were train tracks on one side and a big field on the other. All alone out there, in terms of traffic, and we came upon this field. It was mostly tall grass—might have been a failed crop of something, maybe abandoned, I don't know. A line of bare trees at the far edge, thin gray branches like a fence made out of skeleton hands. Looking through, you could see a small farmhouse set back on its land. Then, as if from the fingers of those hands, a wave of starlings rose up; thousands moving as one body, like black water coming to a boil, blotting out the sky over the field. I pulled to the shoulder, shut the car off, got Mazie unbuckled, stood leaning against the car, holding her tight in my arms, her head on my shoulder and both of us dumbstruck staring at all these birds swooping and maneuvering, sometimes descending back into the branches but never letting more than a few seconds pass before they rose up again, and always together, all as one. Up and back down and back up and they just kept going. It looked to me like they didn't know whether they were free or stuck.

A NIGHT OUT

... and a story called "The Light of the World" which
nobody else ever liked.
—Hemingway, "Preface to 'The First Forty-nine'"

Caleb is good-looking and something of a fashionista—
whatever that means. You're not sure, but it's the word you
think of when you think of your old friend who these days blogs
album reviews for a national fashion magazine and writes art
reviews for a print-only underground literary annual called—
for no reason you can discern—*Farm Report*. Back in August,
for your golden birthday, i.e., the day one turns the same age as
one's date of birth—twenty-nine on the twenty-ninth, in your
case—Caleb got you each an eight ball and took you out for a
crosstown spree: the Maritime Hotel, the Jane, a pit stop at the

Spotted Pig for burgers before heading to the LES—"*Lush Life*
land," quoth Caleb, never one to shrink from irony though it's a
safe bet he hasn't read the book.

You finally cabbed it home at sunrise, slept clear through the
afternoon, and woke up to a prodigious nosebleed—straight-up
terror, fucking swimming in your own blood—itself the herald of a sinus disaster that swelled your whole face up and kept
you out of the office for three days. Two weeks of antibiotics,
little souvenir lump of scar tissue in your right cheek—too small
to see unless someone's looking real close, but you can feel it
with your thumb and sometimes when you're nervous you'll
catch yourself worrying it back and forth like a pebble under a
beach towel. So obviously you swore off cocaine forever—lesson
learned, thanks—and yet for some reason hung onto the still-
mostly-full bag. It's been in the drawer of your bedside table for
five-plus months. You're getting ready to go meet Caleb at his
place; then together you'll head over to Sandra's party.

Lindsey's at a Chelsea gallery, breaking her own first rule of art
openings: never order the special original-recipe cocktail. The
bartender is invariably somebody's assistant/boyfriend/nephew
and he doesn't know how to make this drink, or any drink more
complicated than, say, a screwdriver. He's reading the recipe
for the nth time off the smeary 3x5 it's scrawled on. He doesn't
"get" measurements. He's worried about his hair. But Lindsey
has a thing for Goldschläger and so she breaks the rule and now
she's got this gallery-monogrammed rocks glass full of bracing
poison: cinnamon and citrus (fucking Christ, is that grapefruit

juice?), gold flakes suspended in pink pulp. She swipes at her watering eyes with a downy blond forearm. When her vision clears she's staring at a wall-size blowup of the same arm she just raked across her face.

This is her friend Logan's show so he must be here somewhere. Last year he got this idea that he would try to sexualize apparently neutral parts of women's bodies, napes of necks and backs of knees and things. Lindsey wanted to—but didn't—say that a woman's body doesn't have any neutral parts, but when Logan asked her to model for him she grudgingly agreed. He took high-res close-ups, pinned the prints right onto the edges of his easel. Then he got—his words—"painter's block." He stared at the photos for days, for weeks, the brush in his unmoving hand, unable to begin. He ended up having the photographs themselves blown up and mounted on foam boards, then called his gallerist, ecstatic, and then all of the girls, most of whom readily consented to the change of plans. Lindsey wound up being the lone holdout, because she's always been weird about her arm hair, but she let Logan convince her that this wasn't just about him, his project and career, but in fact represented an opportunity for Lindsey in the form of personal growth. Anyway here she is up there, wrist to elbow, her freckles big as skulls, her forearm down a forest of white-gold light.

Lindsey's about halfway through her cocktail. Phone's buzzing in her purse. She steps outside to take the call and it's Sandra wanting to know when she's coming to her birthday party. "You're one of my go-to girls, Linz," Sandra's saying. "I need you here early so it looks like something when everyone else

gets here." A pause. "And so I'm not fucking drinking alone."
Lindsey rolls her eyes but says OK, sure, she's on the way. Who
knows, maybe Caleb will be there. Sort of weird, come to think
of it, that she didn't run into him here. She texts Logan to tell
him she's so sorry they missed each other, steps into the street,
hails a cab. She slides in and says, "SoHo." The art world slips
into the rearview mirror as she gags on a gulp of her pink drink
and realizes, shit, she's stolen the glass. If the cabbie notices he
doesn't let on.

Sandra is petite and so beautiful she's sometimes hard to look
at, particularly when she does this quasi-Egyptian thing with
her eyeliner. As it happens, today, the thirtieth, is her golden
birthday. It's January.

Via Caleb, you've met Sandra once or twice before. Was she
maybe there on your birthday, at one of the bars or another?
Odds are. She's nice enough, aloof though, and you aren't wild
about the crowd she runs with. In fact, you had to be talked into
going to this thing at all. You'd been thinking, Night in; thinking, Netflix Instant and takeout. But Caleb seemed to want you
here—need you here, almost, though Caleb never quite needs
anything. When you remembered what was in your drawer,
some weird counterintuition sensor in your mind got tripped;
you fished the bag out of a cuff links box and tucked it into that
part of your wallet where condoms go.

Caleb doesn't like to smoke in his own apartment—filthy
habit, he says—so you guys are on the roof of his building, eight
or nine stories up, in that part of the East Village that stayed

rough into the mid-'90s but then caved in and got safe like everything else. You're hoping he'll finish before the warming flush of the drugs does, at which point you'll start to feel the chill. Above you the night sky is swollen and gray-white.

Sandra has a long-term boyfriend, Gene—away on tour like usual. As far as anyone can tell, she's faithful to him. His band doesn't have an album yet, but ever since they got a song on the soundtrack to the summer's second-biggest superhero movie they've been getting pride of place in the "favorite bands" category on the social network profiles of all the country's coolest skater tweens. Caleb—like any good heterosexual friend to a stunning, untouchable woman—has been valiantly sleeping his way through Sandra's Rolodex.

A lot of people think Caleb's an operator, man slut, etc., and there's a case to be made there, sure, but you happen to know that Caleb loves Sandra, she's the one for him, because Caleb has just said so, in exactly those saccharine and hackneyed terms, which is in its way as shocking as the sentiment itself.

Caleb in profile, Gauloise between his lips (he brings back cartons every time he goes to Paris), dark glasses on, collar of his leather jacket popped. You're a couple lines in now and thinking how if you tried to describe Caleb to anyone who didn't know him the guy would sound like a total poseur blowhard but that would be such bullshit because Caleb is the real deal in the sense that the life he appears to be living—whatever you might think of it—is the actual life that he lives, not an imitation of something he read about on the Internet or only has time for on the weekend—and the lesson is, well, you're not totally sure, but it's along the lines of that nobody should judge anyone, and hell, who do you think you are, anyway? You wear a tie all day. Wing tips, Christ almighty, to an office in a building on Maiden Lane. We're all cartoon versions of ourselves.

Caleb flicks the cigarette over the roof edge, leans out to witness its earthward flutter, wobbles on his heels, and you're bolting across the roof, grabbing a fistful of jacket, pulling your friend back to safety.

"Dude," Caleb says to you. "Chill."

The SoHo loft is owned, you think, by a friend of a friend of Sandra's who isn't here, or nobody's seen him. Or maybe it's rock star Gene's loft? Whatever. The place is cavernous, moodily track-lit. In one area of the hangar-like room, a digital projector and a MacBook sit side by side on top of a vintage dark wood chest. The projector casts a blazing black-and-white square that sweeps the full sixteen feet from ceiling to floor. You know it's Hitchcock, but you can't place which one. Ingrid Bergman in doctor's whites, older men in suits all around her in what looks like a drawing room. The movie's muted—dance music issues from a dozen hidden speakers, the room suffused in throb.

Elsewhere in the loft, away from the glow of the screen, a pair of Caleb's one-offs are having a chat. He hasn't noticed. Sandra doesn't exactly condone how he is with her friends, but neither has she jerked his leash. Her shows of displeasure and indulgence are understated—as with any queen, her seemingly clearest signals often misdirect and her true desires can only be inferred. You and Caleb are sipping drinks and shooting the speedy breeze while his gaze runs recon routes over the room—who's here? what's up?—and oh, hey, shit, there's that special little clique of two.

"That's not gonna be good for business," he says, and you reply by reflex: "That's not gonna be good for anybody." (Are you two really doing a *Seinfeld* bit? At this party?) Then Lindsey hauls off and slaps Candi in the face, flips a bird clear across the room at Caleb, storms off. Candi's standing dumbfounded, her own hands slack at her sides—not even testing the presumably tender spot on her pinking cheek.

"Do you think it's the fault of the movies that we imagine our lives as movies?" Caleb says as you hustle over.

"I think it's the fault of movies that we imagine ourselves as the stars of our movies," you reply. You guys could riff like this all night but cut yourselves short as you arrive at Candi, who springs to sudden sullen life.

"I just got slapped," she says. "In the face."

"Lindsey seemed pretty upset," Caleb says. "Do you think I should go after her?"

"But I just got slapped," Candi says. "In the face."

"Look," Caleb says, then says nothing. He does look, though—at you. Then he bolts.

"Heya," you say to Candi.

"In the face," she says.

Sandra appears. "Everything OK?"

"Well, well," you say, thrilled to have backup or relief or whatever. "It's the star. Happy golden." Wait. Are you not supposed to know she's thirty? Isn't that the age when you're supposed to stop talking about a woman's age? But maybe phrasing it in the cute terms of the whole golden birthday thing makes it somehow OK.

"I just got slapped," Candi says, and Sandra says, "Oh, Candi, you know how Lindsey gets."

"Yeah, well, and we all know why."

You don't know why, of course, which Sandra must be realizing because she turns purposefully toward you and says, "Thank you," presumably for having wished her a happy birthday, though you feel like that was conversational aeons ago. Now what is Sandra saying?

" . . . two know each other?"

"Drew," you say.

"Candi. But you can call me Slapped in the Face."

"Think of it as a conversation piece," Sandra says. You suspect this has already crossed Candi's mind. You say, "Uh, do either of you want, like—" You put an index finger flush to the side of your nose, make a snort noise, and, inexplicably to the women, wince both of your eyes shut. Your enthusiastic pantomime seems to include a bit of sense memory.

"Thanks," Sandra says, "but not for years now. Getting up there, you know?" Shit. Is that a dig on what you said before? "But if I know Candi here—"

"What was your name again?" Candi asks you. "I'm sorry, I'm a little jostled. I mean—"

"Yeah," you say. "Nobody likes to be slapped in the face."

"Sometimes I wonder," Sandra says, which you're pretty sure was meant for only you to hear, so you're like, what, friends now? Trading digs on your other friends. OK. Or was it some sort of cryptic warning? (Though if it was a warning, it wasn't all that cryptic.) Anyway Sandra's off to make her rounds. She's got her hair up. She even walks like a queen.

"So you were saying," Candi says.

"Was I?"

She mimics your gesture from a moment ago, emphasizing the snort but skipping the wince.

"Gotcha."

Well, you're not gonna do it in front of everyone, and the line for the bathroom is backed up to the edge of the dance floor, so you suggest going downstairs, prop the front door with a rock or something, share a cig. You can bump off your keys when the street's empty. Candi says, "That's pretty ghetto, dude," but in a kind of laughing way that suggests an additional, un-spoken clause: But what do I care? So now you're huddled in a recess between two buildings, not so much an alley as an alcove, a niche. So cold your fingers barely function, your breath and her breath rich white puffs melding into one cloud: there and gone and there again. "We're all living in each other's breath all the time," you say, "only nobody thinks of it like that when they can't see it." A gentleman, you hold the bag for her and she takes the key. Her shoulders are bare. It's a strapless dress, black. She's shivering. At first you aren't sure you see it, but there, in the casts of the streetlights—the fat flakes wink in the glow—it's snowing. Wasn't it supposed to be too cold to snow tonight? You're at the point where pretty much anything seems like a sign. She's beautiful, and everything else is, too. You lay a warming arm across her shoulders. "Let's get out of here," you say. But the coats, duh.

"You go up," she says. "If I go it'll be half an hour with good-byes."

In the cab you kiss and pet a little and sip from a red plastic cup full of strong rum and Coke because you, when you were upstairs, had the good sense to make a drink. Candi, truth be told, is sort of gulping her share. You're both imagining the city as a thing whizzing past you, rather than you through it, though the misconception is a moot point inasmuch as your cab is crawling through traffic, now stopping for a light. Why is this guy trying to go through Union Square? He should have gone west on Houston and taken 6th. Not worth getting into. Your hand riding up Candi's thigh. She leans past you to reach for the party cup.

In the elevator your pupils get so dilated you can barely make each other out through the haze of glare. Your one-bedroom is tiny, but decent for Hell's Kitchen. "Don't turn the light on," she says. She has this certainty about her that's unnerving. She's walking around your dark apartment like she's been coming here for years.

She throws her bag next to the couch, coat on top of the bag, steps out of her heels. She's walking toward the bath—no, bedroom. She's got a hand behind her back, trying to get at the dress's zipper. Shit, if this is how she wants it, well, OK. You take your shoes off, start pulling at your clothes as you walk after her. You drop your belt, decide you should hit the bathroom, pee, splash your face with cold water, lean down into the sink and guzzle. Then you give yourself a few quick strokes, just to check—not that you're one of those guys with an, ahem, problem, but on a night like this it's better to be sure. Anyway, it perks right up, so OK. Great. Sweet. Now save it for game time.

Candi hasn't quite gotten the dress off. The bottom is hiked up to her waist, and the top is pulled halfway down her torso so her breasts are exposed. The Hula-Hoop: classic. She's on her side, facing away from you. You lie down and spoon up to her, try to slip between her legs, but she won't open, not even a little. Too soon? Never can tell what a woman will think is proper procedure. You grab a handful of breast.

What the hell is that?

It's small, about the size of the first pad of your middle finger. A scab? No, it's . . . squishy. In your mind you run through the old health-class list. Never heard of anything like this. A deformity? Some weird giant mole? OK. Shit. What do you do? Should you ask? Does it hurt her when you touch it? Doesn't seem to. You should seriously stop touching it, though. You touch it again.

She's sleeping of course. Has been since she hit the mattress. You're getting that now. On top of everything else, you're feeling up the passed-out girl. Man, this night.

You roll Candi over as gently as you can. The first thing you see—stomach plummet—is that whatever it is is black. And there's one on each breast. For a second you're sure it's leprosy.

But the strapless dress—duh, you fucking asshole. It's tape.

Sweet relief! Now with that settled, let's get back to the issue. How can a person with all that coke in her system be sleeping?

Hmm. Well, there's how much she drank for one thing. Christ, these people and their lives. And if she was ready to pass out, what the hell did she agree to come over for? Caleb owes you big-time for this. Somehow, you feel, this is all your friend's fault. And where is Caleb now? Probably at an after-hours dance club, making up with Lindsey. They'll fuck at sunrise. He'll pretend she's Sandra.

You watch Candi sleep for a minute—kind of checking her out, kind of making sure she keeps breathing—then go into the living room. Snow's still coming down out there. You remember that this meant something to you before, but now you can't remember—can't even guess—what it might have been. Like looking into a mirror and only seeing the mirror (cf. Peck to Bergman in *Spellbound*, which, duh, was what was screening at the party). Your eyes ache; your hands are shaking. You go to the hall closet and find yourself a blanket. It's soft. You wrap yourself up, then hear your phone buzzing in the pocket of your pants, wherever you left those—the hallway. That'll be Caleb wondering where you and the coke are at because he knows that with you holding the bag there'll still be some left. Lucky sonof-abitch is probably with Lindsey and Sandra. So you know what? Just this once, fuck him. You stretch out on the couch, struggle to push Caleb's presumed ménage from your mind, then jerk off while thinking about Candi's tits and what you saw and briefly groped of her legs and ass. Not your finest hour to be sure, but at least you're not standing in there, mouth-breathing over her. You go into the bathroom, finish directly into the toilet, flush, collapse back to the couch, and fall quickly into deep but worthless sleep. When you wake up it's the next day and she's long, long gone.

Caleb finds Lindsey in the stairwell.

She starts to kiss him. He kisses back for a minute, then remembers how he promised himself he wouldn't do this. Tonight is his night with Sandra. He extracts himself from Lindsey. There's some crying but not much. Having slapped Candi, Lindsey feels like she's made her point and could truthfully take or leave getting laid. Caleb's good, but he's also old news. She lets him go. He's back inside, walking past a little cluster of people who are still talking about the slap.

"Yeah," some guy is saying, "but crazy girls are a lot of fun." Two of his buddies agree. The first guy makes an engine-growl noise, like *vrrroww*, i.e., sex stuff. One girl doesn't think it's funny. Her name is Amy, Caleb seems to know. "Crazy girls," Amy says, "ruin things for everybody. Especially for not-crazy girls."

To Caleb this remark instantly pegs Amy as the smartest person here. Sandra is not a crazy person. He is going to win her heart. He makes a drink. He crosses the room. He sees you come in, grab two coats, pour an insane-looking rum and Coke, leave again. *Hey, all right*, he thinks. *Good for him—guy could use a little fun in his life.*

There's a DJ doing the music now, some skinny bald guy supposedly semifamous on the West Coast, hunched over a pair of turntables with USB ports hooked into a brushed aluminum MacBook Pro. Sampled snatches of music are like flying fish in the river of a doubled-up dubstep, breaking the surface and flashing in the air, then disappearing again. Sandra's dancing with Lindsey and Caleb wants to join in. He's an incredible dancer but has always held back around Sandra because dancing means ceding control over his instincts—usually a plus, but when he's around Sandra he needs to maintain exquisite control. Ahh, these girls! They're both so perfect. They shine. How can he even watch them, much less join in? How can he not?

Suddenly Sandra stops dancing. She's seen something. For a second Caleb thinks it's him and they're having a moment—maybe *the* moment—but then he realizes no, her eyes are looking past his, past him. Perhaps you and Candi are back from wherever you guys snuck off to, which he figures was the roof. But you've only been gone for—well, time's become sort of a nebulous concept here in Caleb Land, and anyway back to the main issue, which is, What—who—is Sandra looking at? All he has to do is turn his body around.

Sandra, thrilled, squealing: "Gene! You made it!"

Now Caleb's on the roof with a bottle of Maker's, looking for you and Candi and the bag. But what the fuck, man? There's nobody up here. Swig. God, snow's annoying. He's sitting on this stumpy metal thing. The whole roof is white. It's still coming down. *I spend a lot of my life on rooftops,* Caleb thinks. *What, if anything, does this mean?* Of course, to parse this question Caleb would need to concede the premise of a world where meaning is (a) possible and (b) desirable, both notions antithetical to him. He drops the line of thought like a kid bored with a toy, flips his cell phone open, sends you that text message you ignored. Swig.

There's a sort of jump cut in his mind, or maybe a whole scene's missing. There was nearly half a bottle, now there's nothing. The world swirls, sparkling, falling. Where's his jacket? Fuck it. He closes his eyes and the dark swirls, too.

Sandra is in Gene's arms, her own arms tight around his neck, squeezing out *Sogoodtoseeyou* and *Babynevergonnaletyougo*. She's been sipping Belvedere since sunset and feeling nothing; it passes through her blood like water, or so she thought, but now, here, as his hands find her narrow hips and circle them it's like— hello! She realizes she's barely on her feet, and all of that Emma- and-Mr.-Knightley bullshit with Caleb is instantly vaporized. Not to say that she doesn't feel for him—indeed, she feels for all of them, every person at the party, their names chant through her thrilling and woozing brain: Caleb, Lindsey, Candi, Mark, Miles, Brandon, Amy, Alec, Shannon, Teresa, that friend of Ca- leb's, uh . . . she's trying to remember your name but then gives up because why bother? Gene is here! Gene who keeps kissing her, and she will let him prolong the moment for however long he wishes—has it been mere seconds? a whole minute yet? who knows—but she can't help opening her eyes for a quick survey of the party around her and she sees Caleb storm out the door, holding the fat-bottomed Maker's bottle by its long neck coated in carmine wax; it swings briskly in time with his furious stride. On the one hand, how dare he! On the other—well, everything. She'll deal with him after Gene goes away again; late next week, she thinks. Truth is, if Caleb would out-and-out come on to her, she'd probably go for it, palace intrigue being SOP for a palace, after all, besides which who knows (better not to dwell on this) what Gene gets up to on the road. But in order to take the queen you have to have guts enough to make a play for her, so what's left to even say?

Lindsey's back in Chelsea at the after-party for Logan's show. They're in this restaurant on 10th Avenue that's got a cobblestone patio—terrace? courtyard?—with what looks like a nobullshit oak tree planted in its center, but of course it's like five degrees and snowing so nobody's out there. She's on an oxblood banquette between Logan and some middle-aged guy wearing a white silk vest over a blue silk shirt tucked into a pair of black dad jeans. The gallerist introduces them, explains in tones of dulcet condescension that Vest is now the proud owner of Lindsey's arm. Lindsey offers what she hopes is a winning smile as she obliges Vest's request for "a closer look at the real thing." He takes her arm in his hands, lifts and bends it for different angles. Logan, below the table, puts a hand on Lindsey's knee, squeezes. The gesture is meant, she thinks, to communicate some combination of "Thank you" and "I'm sorry" because they've talked a million times before about how awful it is that he has to suck up to assholes like Vest, but how it's part of the game, inescapable, way of the world, etc. Anyway his hand is a comfort, even if it does seem to be migrating north. Vest, meanwhile, keeps one-handed hold of her elbow while he knocks back his vodka cran, then announces that he's going to count her freckles. She doesn't bother to tell him he's holding the wrong arm, turns her attention back to Logan, who is unsuccessfully attempting to work his fingers between her tightly crossed thighs. *This*, she thinks, *is when all that fucking yoga pays off.*

Lindsey wonders if Logan's show sold out and, if so, how much money he made. She forgot to look at any of the prices when she was there earlier. She wonders what Vest paid for her arm, thinks of asking him, changes her mind. The gallerist is handing a credit card to the waiter. Vest releases her arm, turns to a girl across the table, another one of Logan's models, asks her which part of her he "missed the chance to cherish forever." The girl doesn't say anything, just leans forward until her forehead is pressed to the table, grabs a fistful of her own hair from the back of her head to pull it out of the way, with the other hand points to the pale mound where her neck becomes her spine.

Candi's back in the orange room with the tall door so ghostly pale purple that it might be gray. This is where her brain sends her whenever she blacks out. She kind of wants to call it her "safe place" only she can't say she feels very safe here. It's a creepy purgatory cluttered with stuff—furniture? objects?—all rendered in this weird skeleton geometry so she can't tell what she's looking at, indeed feels she is perhaps not even in the room but merely viewing it, as though it were not a place at all but a picture, a canvas or a page, but if that's true then why is she able to walk across the orange floor toward the tall door, to reach her hand out for the knob and, watching her fingers pass through it, wonder whether it is she or the room that is ethereal? Here, as ever, is where the dream begins to deflate, as though it were a balloon pricked by the pin of her uncertainty.

Now she's awake in an unfamiliar bedroom in a hiked-up (and pulled-down) black dress. The good news is her underwear's still on; there don't seem to be stains on the sheets. In the living room, that semicute guy with the drugs from the party—i.e., you—is asleep on what she rightly infers is your own couch. You're tangled in a blanket with a throw pillow over your face to block out the morning sun. Huge chunks of her night are missing, but it's clear enough what must have happened. There's a red Solo cup on your kitchen counter. She can see from where she's standing that it's empty.

If she wakes you you might take her out to breakfast. That'd be nice, but it'd also mean at least an hour of chitchat. She starts to look for your wallet or a piece of mail, anything with your name on it, then changes her mind and decides to bail. Better to be mysterious. If you're even halfway interested in her you'll ask Caleb for her number. Speaking of which, her phone's battery apparently ran out of juice at some point last night. Oops.

The plows have already come through; snow piles stand waist-high. The stretches of sidewalk between the driveways are like little canyons. Her heels click on that synthetic salt stuff they throw down. The gutters aren't even muddy yet; it hasn't been light out long enough. Everything looks pure in that superficial way. Snow.

She sees a cab and hails it, gets in, fastens her seatbelt, then gives him the address. If she'd told him first he'd have peeled out and left her standing there. He shakes his head, about as annoyed as she expected, but punches the address into his GPS and pulls back into traffic. He resumes his conversation—in

Gujarati or whatever—with whoever's on the other end of the Bluetooth clipped to his left ear. She puts her forehead against the cold window. Looking at all the early commuters and other cars and changing scenery is nauseating. She shuts her eyes and tries to lose herself in the hum and shake of the car. She's dozing but only lightly, having one of those dreams about being exactly where you are.

Candi has the keys to her sister's place but knocks before she lets herself in. Taya is standing in the hall where it meets the kitchen—these Windsor Terrace brownstones, you get space out here—holding her daughter, Emily, on a cocked hip. Taya takes one look. "Where did you sleep last night?"

Over coffee, Candi tells her story, embroidering as she goes—what everyone was wearing, what the coke must have cost, the whole backstory of why Lindsey slapped her. She fills in the big gaps with lurid surmises and fibs. In her telling, you get six inches taller, are wearing brands Caleb favors (you've never heard of them), and are the bassist in Gene's band. Taya's pitch-perfect in her big-sister act: mildly disapproving but also obviously jealous—everything Candi hoped for. Her sister is the best.

They decide to call their mother, who lives upstate and is always going on about some new herbal weight-loss drug she ordered off the TV. "You won't be young forever, girls," her mother likes to say in this evil little singsong, and ain't that the truth? Though the lesson Candi takes from the admonition is not to stock up on diet pills and join a Pilates class but rather to get her kicks in while she can.

After Emily talks to Grandma she says she wants to go to the park. Taya says it's too cold to go but Emily won't stop talking about it, so Candi says she'll take her and they get the kid dressed. Candi, too—she roots around in her sister's closet. Their sizes run close enough. Taya says she'll bake banana bread while they're gone.

"Oh, I almost forgot, I need to charge my phone."

"No prob. I'll plug yours in and you can take mine just in case."

At the playground, the swings and slide have been mostly erased by the snowfall. Emily's zipped up and insulated, crash-proof, so Candi lets her go wild among the vague shapes. A flyer taped to a streetlight reads, REJOICE—YOU ARE A REALLY SPECIAL PERSON IN THE HEART OF GOD AND HIS PERFECT PLAN HAS A UNIQUE PLACE IN IT JUST FOR YOU. She pulls her sister's heavy coat tight around herself, plunges into the snow to catch up with her niece.

THE HAPPY VALLEY

Danielle had her days to herself and half the summer still in front of her. A Fodor's guide and a debit card called the Octopus, Hong Kong's version of a rail pass, but you could use it in cabs, too, and even some stores. She ate noodles in steaming broth at the last dai pai dong in Wan Chai, was given scissors to shell squillas with at a food stall in North Point Market. She slurped xiao long bao—soup dumplings—at the Victoria Harbour Restaurant in what had once been a waterfront property but now, thanks to the ongoing "harbor reclamation" project, was several bustling city blocks inland from its namesake. Everywhere she looked, it seemed, new buildings were being constructed while old ones were under renovation or being razed. The city never stopped changing, never slowed. Hong Kong truly was the city that New York claimed to be, she thought, a bit guiltily, even though she hadn't exactly meant it as praise. She could not accustom herself to the sight of the lashed bamboo they used for scaffolding here, but at least the workers didn't catcall, or if they did their words were lost in the language gap, as were most billboards, street chatter, and whatever was on the radio in a given taxi or store. So many pretty colors, so much white noise.

Cold air blasted from the open-faced storefronts as she made her way along Nathan Road, Kowloon's main tourist drag. She was awed by the flagrant waste even as she moved to the inside of the sidewalk to make sure she didn't miss a single hit of chill. She imagined electric bills in quantum notation. She rode the funicular, the ding-ding, the double-decker bus out to Shek O once, but never the red-and-green minibuses; those things were death traps, her father had warned: the worst.

She went to the historic markets—bird, flower, fish, and jade. She stood in front of the Chungking Mansions, let the hustlers' pitches wash over her. She did not want to follow them to where their knockoff purses and watches were cached. She did not want to eat at their brothers' food stalls. She stood on the viewing platform on the roof of the mall at the Peak. She went to the racetrack in the Happy Valley and bet on the horses with the names she liked best: Bespoke Master, Cars King Prawn. In the high distance beyond the grandstand, above the colonial cemetery, stood a pair of blue-glass residential towers everyone called "the chopsticks." They looked like twins but weren't.

She spent an afternoon at the JCC on Robinson Road. They had a library and were happy to let her use it even though she wasn't a member. Danielle read about the prominent families,

Sassoons and Kadoories, how they came over with the British from Baghdad and owned merchant shops and founded charities and later opened the Peninsula Hotel. She read about the Axis occupation, how most Jews fled to Shanghai and the island's oldest synagogue was turned into stables and all the British subjects were sent to prison camps. She shared these stories with her father over dinner at a Lebanese restaurant, their first proper meal together in three or four days.

"Did you know that Nathan Road is named for the first Jewish governor of Hong Kong?" Danielle asked. She did not mention that in the ninety years between Sir Matthew Nathan's reassignment to South Africa and Hong Kong's return to Chinese control there had never been another Jew in charge. Her father had always enjoyed history, and over the years had developed a bombastic pride in his heritage—this despite a near-perfect indifference to its teachings or practice. This was common among Jewish men in their late middle age, Danielle thought; she had many friends whose fathers had done the same. Stan Ross seemed to believe he held claim to a share of the credit for anything any of their people had ever accomplished, individually or collectively, including living in a given place for any length of time without being annihilated or kicked out. Which is why the Jewish history of Hong Kong had seemed like such a promising topic, the very thing to draw him out of what Danielle took to be his abiding stoicism, a term she preferred to the other options that suggested themselves: reticence, dissatisfaction, boredom, gloom. But she hadn't anticipated that they'd be having the conversation in this particular venue. A Lebanese restaurant might well be the den of the enemy, for all they knew, though the artwork on the walls suggested Coptic Christianity, which in turn probably meant these people were more rabidly pro-Israel than even her father was. Still, he wasn't certain, and said he meant to maintain his ignorance so he could keep eating here in good conscience, or at least not in bad. There were a hundred places to get shawarma in Hong Kong but this one was his favorite; they had a house-made spicy ketchup that he all but ate straight with a spoon. His suit jacket hung on the back of his chair. He'd taken his gold cuff links out, rolled his sleeves up almost to his elbows.

A plate of baklava was brought to the table. They hadn't ordered it but happily tucked in. A few minutes later the owner emerged from the back. A thick man with olive skin and a creased face, wearing a sauce-spotted apron over a golf shirt and chinos. Danielle's father stood to greet him. The men shook hands, called each other by their first names. Danielle stood up also, cleared her throat. "This is my daughter," her father said, turning toward her and making a small gesture of introduction with his hands.

"Ahh, so wonderful," the man said. "A daughter. I had no idea."

In Sha Tin she walked the concrete path uphill toward the Temple of Ten Thousand Buddhas. The Fodor's said the project had been undertaken in 1949, the infancy of the post-war, and completed in '57, the same year her father was born. Was this history then? Buddhas lined both sides of the path, life-size on red pedestals that doubled as planters. They sat amid greenery and behind them rows of trees reached twenty, thirty, forty feet up like canyon walls. The Buddhas were bald of course, but most of them were skinny, which was a surprise. Excepting their black swoop eyebrows and crimson lips they were gold from head to toe. Many were tranquil, reserved, dignified, but others had wild expressions and seemed alive with anger or sorrow; some appeared to leer. The farther Danielle walked, the higher she climbed, and the more ornate the Buddhas became. They held staves and lotuses, boasted haloes and filigreed robes, rode animal familiars, wielded swords. Some were freaks. One stood eight feet tall on Gumby legs. Another had white eyebrows so long they coiled ropelike in his lap. Her favorite had a black Fu Manchu framing pursed lips, a blue cap that matched his robe, and muscular baby arms growing out of his eye sockets. On the hands of these arms, thumbs were pressed to third fingers as if in meditation. Small colorless eyes like cauterized wounds stared out from the proffered palms.

Stan Ross had come out to Hong Kong with Lehman Brothers but by the time the shit hit the fan with the market he'd left the company to start his own thing. Ross Investments was a fund that specialized in mainland Chinese real estate. He got the rights to things—lands, development deals—that were next to impossible for non-Chinese citizens to get the rights to. What could not be done, he did. He had divorced his wife, Lynne, when Danielle was a junior in high school, five—no, six—years ago and left the States maybe two years after that. When Lynne took her maiden name of Melman back Danielle insisted on taking it, too. She saw her father when he came stateside on business, once or twice a year. He'd build a few extra days into his schedule, rent a car in New York, and drive out to the Pioneer Valley: see the college, take her and her girlfriends out to dinner, shake hands with whichever indifferent boy she threw in front of him, weather her moods. If he so much as mentioned her mother she turned to stone. It wasn't until Lynne got engaged to Cliff that Danielle realized she was the last man standing on the battlefield of her parents' marriage—the war was over, won and lost, and there she was in the smoking ruins, waving a flag. Why? Because she'd been doing it so long she didn't know what else to do, how else to be with her father. Their relationship had narrowed to her anger at him. She finished school at the beginning of May, and her mother's wedding was in Peekskill on Memorial Day weekend. The following Tuesday, the three of them drove to the airport together. Mr. and Mrs. Cliff Sutphen had gone to Majorca for twelve days and Danielle, still a Melman—now the only Melman—had come here for the summer.

Her father's apartment was on the far south side of the island in the Repulse Bay, a combination hotel and residence. The building was baby blue with yellow and peach highlights, long and skinny like a flag. The paint job reminded her of downtown Miami but the rolling lawns and white stone walkways were straight colonial nostalgia chic. Across the street were the bay and its half-moon beach. Her dad said the design of the Repulse Bay epitomized Hong Kong logic: a modern luxury building for the international business and leisure class but built with a several-stories-high feng shui hole through its middle to ensure that the dragon who lived in the mountain still had access to the water.

The sunsets were incredible. Air pollution blown down from Shenzhen warped the light into something out of Coleridge—blustery, beautiful, unreal. She often went down to watch from the sand, would look away from the water and back through the hole in the hotel to the green slope dissolving in shadow. In her mind she saw the dragon blazing through the gap like a rocket, leaving hot wake behind him in his plunge from the mountain to the sea.

Ross Investments was developing golf courses across the Chinese countryside, the logic being that as the Chinese middle class inevitably suburbanized itself in the American style (which to them would, presumably, not seem stultifying or hopelessly quaint) the courses—and the roads that led to the courses—would make natural anchors for housing developments. Her father was forever taking trips to meet with businessmen or view promising sites. Danielle regarded her father broadly as a visionary. At the same time she found his particular vision unsettling, even ugly. But if he didn't do these things surely somebody else would. She tried to love her father unconditionally, even as she was coming to understand that she hardly knew him. She knew he was considered an innovator in his field, that he liked shawarma with spicy ketchup. She knew what his iPod was loaded with—Clapton, Hendrix, Eagles, Beatles, Stones—but she had never seen him listening to it. He didn't always remember to take it when he went on trips. She knew he preferred the elliptical to the treadmill, but only exercised at all because his doctor had advised it. She knew that the woman who wrecked his marriage—or, rather, for whom he'd wrecked his own marriage—was named Erica, but that their thing had ended well before he'd moved to Asia, and that he seemed to have been alone since then, or at least to be alone now. She knew he always took his golf clubs with him when he went to Beijing.

There was a Thai restaurant in a small shack at the edge of the beach. Danielle ordered pad Thai and a spring roll—unimaginative choices, perhaps, but her favorite—and took her dinner down to the sand. She had a blanket and a bottle of wine in her satchel: a sweet, lonely sunset picnic. There wasn't usually anyone out at this hour, but today she spotted a family on their way back from a walk along the shore. At first they were silent silhouettes, but as they got closer she could hear the little boy's *vroom* noises, could see that he was kicking up sand and tearing away from his parents, careening ahead. The man let go of his wife's hand and started to jog after his son, but he was a beat too late. The kid had already closed the distance, hopped right over Danielle's wine bottle, and landed in her arms.

"Aunt Rachel!" he said. He was American. She hugged him back.

"Hi there," she said to him while looking over his head at his dad.

"I'm so sorry," the dad said to Danielle. And to his son, "Dylan, honey, that's not Aunt Rachel." To Danielle again: "I'm so sorry. You look, it's actually funny, kind of like a friend of ours. She lives in the States, Dylan knows her from Skype, and we've been telling him how she's coming to visit later this summer and—well." He shrugged and grinned, as in, You know how kids can be. Dylan was pudgy and warm—she could feel his heart humming in his chest against hers. The man stepped onto Danielle's blanket. He leaned in close. She could smell his cologne or else deodorant, felt his strong fingers slide between her body and his son's. Dylan giggled as he was pulled from Danielle's arms, found himself hoisted up onto his father's shoulders. "Ellen," the man said, turning away from Danielle and toward his wife, who was still a few yards off. "Honey, you're gonna get a kick out of this."

Before he took his most recent leave, Danielle had complained of her loneliness to her father. She felt isolated, she said, hoping he might cancel his trip or invite her along. Neither of those options, he explained, was feasible. But if she liked he could e-introduce her to some of his employees, people with whom she might, in his words, "have something in common." By this Danielle thought he meant that they were in their thirties, most of them, which she supposed was better than nothing. Back upstairs, the memory of the boy's warmth and the man's grazing fingers still faintly on her skin, Danielle fired off a BBM to the one named Colin. She had her fingers crossed he'd turn out to be English or at least Australian. He pinged back a couple minutes later, said he was out with some people in Lan Kwai Fong and she was welcome to join up if she liked. Danielle rolled her eyes. LKF was an endless expat frat party crammed into a few blocks of bars and restaurants at the edge of downtown. It was like a bizarro Bourbon Street where all of the tourists were finance people and also weren't tourists so the same ones came back every night.

"Cool," she replied. "U got an address?"

"Place called Stormies. White bldg at bend of d'aguilar st elbow. Big pink neon sign, boat theme, u cant miss."

She guessed it would take her a half hour to get there.

"From Repulse that's optimistic," he replied, "but no worries. Here for the long haul." It was a Monday.

Colin was fit and sandy-haired, maybe with some gray mixed in but it was hard to tell. He wore black slacks and black loafers, a white shirt with silver cuff links, his collar and the next button down both open. He was sitting with a small group at a table near the door. "Heya," he said—American; oh well. The bar was a nightmare. When he'd said "boat" she'd thought yacht club, but this was more like Jersey Shore. They were blasting Bon Jovi. People were doing Jell-O shots out of plastic syringes. She hadn't sat down yet and she was ready to leave. Colin leaned in and shouted in her ear: "Comforts of home, eh?" They made her a spot at their table and he made introductions: Rajiv, Hugh, Megan, and Thao. They were all eager to know how Danielle was enjoying her visit, what she'd eaten, where she'd been. She told them about the Buddhas at Sha Tin, then asked how they all knew one another. Colin explained that they all worked together, or rather had worked together until a recent shake-up. Megan had been recruited for executive management and her reconfigured portfolio was taking her out of the division, which itself was being scaled down, as a side effect of which Rajiv had been let go and Hugh was about to announce that he would quit; he was joining Colin, working for Danielle's dad. (One of the things Danielle had learned about expats was that since their jobs were their only reason on earth for being where they were, it was rude not to let them go on a bit about the minutiae of their office lives.) Thao—Vietnamese by way of London and Berlin, though all his degrees were from American schools—believed that he would soon be doing what amounted to both Rajiv's and Hugh's jobs. He was pressing Megan as to whether she thought, in her freshly executive opinion, he might be offered a salary bump and/or new title. Rajiv was going back to Kerala so his in-laws could spend some time with their granddaughter before he moved his family to the States, where he hoped to buy some American real estate before the economy got better and interest rates went back up. So these were not just drinks Danielle had stumbled into but good-bye drinks. But in Hong Kong, Colin said, leaning close again, his lips brushing her ear as he struggled to make himself heard over Bono and then Fred Durst, everyone was always coming or going, so nobody got too worked up. Everything here was a stepping-stone to something else—the Singapore or Beijing office, a new job with a different firm in London or New York or Mumbai or wherever home was or wherever you wanted it to be next.

Danielle stared into her "Dark and Stormie"—the house special, her second or maybe third one—and wanted to say something but didn't know what it was. She wanted to ask them questions about her father, whom she gathered they all knew or at least knew of. Was he open in his dealings, free with his anger, generous with his time? Did he remember people's birthdays? Did he have a girlfriend and what was her name? Had he ever set foot inside this particular awful fucking bar? But none of those questions was the real question, or if one was it would cease to be as soon as she asked it. There was something great and shapeless alive inside her and to speak it would be to distort its essential character. Its truth abided in the fact of its remaining forever suspended, unborn. Danielle drank her drink.

People took their money clips out, started to say their goodbyes. Danielle reached for her purse but they stopped her. She tried to insist but Colin put his hand down on top of hers, said, "Danielle, please." She made a mental note to give a good report to her father, whenever she saw him again.

"I'll see you 'round," they all said to one another, though in several cases there was no particular reason to believe that this was so.

Hugh and Colin, luckily, were still up for action, and Danielle was feeling comfortable enough at this point to tell them what she really thought of LKF, so they hopped in a cab and made for a place on Johnston Road called the Pawn. There were love seats and overstuffed leather chairs clustered around low black tables. They had a walk-in humidor, a whiskey list so long it came in a leather-bound book. Another of her father's employees met them there. Like many native-born Chinese who dealt regularly with Westerners, he'd adopted a Western first name and introduced himself as Ned Chu. They were on a third-floor balcony, the men all sipping Laphroaig 16, Danielle with a Grey Goose and cran.

"This used to be an actual pawn shop," Ned said.

"No shit," Hugh said.

"It's true," Ned continued. "My father was a beat cop in the seventies. He walked these streets every night. Talk about a different world." But then he didn't talk about it, and none of them pressed him. He stared past the railing and out at the busy street, looking at the strolling people and passing cars as if he didn't quite believe in them. Danielle thought of the mountain dragon exploding through the hole in her father's building. Hugh, rolling a pin joint, let out a small contented sigh. "Hong Kong," he said, "is whatever you want whenever you want it, all the time."

"Ask my father about that," Ned said. "I always say to him to write a book." But again, nobody bit. These guys weren't interested in history, Danielle thought. They were barely interested in the present. She felt that this fact explained something essential about who they were or the circles they ran in or the world they were forging, or something, but she couldn't decide whether this essential thing was what made them fundamentally different from her, or whether it was rather the basis for whatever little common ground they shared. Danielle knew one thing: it was a million degrees out and humid as a swamp. She knocked her drink back, shut her eyes against the welcome clatter of ice cubes on her nose.

"How's it going over there?" Colin said.

"Ready to call it a night, I think."

Colin walked her downstairs and hailed her a cab. It crossed Danielle's mind that Colin might share the cab with her, though she doubted they lived near each other. Her father's place wasn't near much of anything. Still. Maybe he'd slide in beside her and see if she balked. That was ridiculous of course, with Ned and Hugh standing right there on the balcony, looking down at them, glasses raised in mock salute. Colin ignored them; Danielle waved back. They stood with the open cab door between them. Colin said, "I'm glad you made it out, Danielle. We should do this again sometime—or something else."

"Yeah," Danielle said. "Let's do whatever we want all the time."

Colin shut the door, put his face up to the window, winked once, then stood upright and slapped his hand on the trunk. The driver hit the gas. Danielle was drunk and alone on the wrong side of the planet, a strange city streaking past a window that might as well have been a movie or computer screen. Or maybe, she thought, the window was a camera and she was the one in the movie: The radio blares Chinese pop music. The pretty girl slumps alone in the backseat as highways yield to mountain roads curving through foreign dark. Cut to:

Danielle woke up hungover, popped a coffee pod into the Keurig, hit the button, held her head while the machine wheezed and clugged. She sat on the porch with her mug and stared out at the bay. It was late morning, hot and hazy. She took a long shower, then went back to sleep. When she woke up there was a BBM from Colin: "Heyagain. Hike this weekend if yr free?"

"Why not tomorrow?" she fired back. "Not like my old man's there to crack the whip."

"Touche but 2morrow no good. Could do thurs tho. Meet at Central Pier, 1230. U need directions?"

"I can always use direction," she wrote. Thinking, *If this doesn't do it . . .*

They took the one o'clock ferry to Lamma Island, disembarked at Yung Shue Wan, a village of seafood restaurants and narrow poured-concrete homes on narrow roads. Men drove puttering flatbeds the size of golf carts, hauling stacks of pressboard and sections of pipe. Frayed strips of sun-bleached tarp rose in the hot breeze like fingers. Construction dust rimed branches and fronds. They walked past cloudy fish tanks full of razor clam, lobster, eel, and prawn.

The walking path would take them south across the ridge of the island along Ha Mei Wan Bay, which was scenic despite a three-stack coal-fired power plant that, like a dark spot on the retina, occupied a small corner of every otherwise perfect view. (Colin said it powered all of Hong Kong—Danielle thought reflexively of the frigid air forever bleeding from the storefronts all over town.)

They made their way out of the village center, wound through the trees, past the mouths of cart-scale driveways that led to tucked-away bungalows. Danielle had a Nalgene in her satchel. She unscrewed the cap, took a big swig, offered the bottle to Colin, who accepted it with evident gratitude. "There's nobody out today," he said as he handed the bottle back to her. "I bet we don't see another person till we get to Sok Kwu Wan."

"Lucky us," Danielle said.

They emerged from the forest—or was it jungle? Or were both these terms too grandiose? Was it maybe just some trees? They mopped their foreheads on their sleeves, walked over green slopes dotted with broken white stones. Danielle said that the landscape felt Scottish and when he laughed at her she faked a little pout. They took the optional detour up Mount Stenhouse and high-fived at the viewing platform, thrilled to have found a vista untroubled by the power plant. Danielle wanted to take a picture together but he got weird about it, like employing the technology of the camera phone would somehow tarnish their experience of nature. She was about to call him out on his affected Luddite bullshit when it occurred to her that he must be worried about people from the office, her father, seeing the picture, so she put her BlackBerry away and finally, finally, he kissed her. They fooled around like high school kids up there at the top of the path.

The descent took them through stinking marshes and more wooded land, then finally into a village that seemed a mirror of the one they'd set out from, though this Tin Hau temple was a little bigger and had a turtle pond. The turtles had red markings on their pointy, wizened heads. They paddled around their oval pool and swam through algae and bumped into lily pads. They hauled themselves slowly from the water. With their webbed feet and small claws they struggled for purchase, then laid themselves out on the hot gray stone.

They took the ferry back to Central, then a cab to Colin's building. In the elevator they saw themselves reflected in the dull gold finish of the doors. Danielle thought they looked like they were trapped in amber. The elevator sighed to a stop and the doors slid open. There were shoes on a rack in the foyer of his apartment: loafers, sandals, little blue sneakers with Velcro straps, a scuffed pair of mary janes. As Danielle knelt to unlace her own sneakers she noticed a framed photograph on the far wall—Colin, a bottle blonde (the eyebrows gave her away), and a little boy. They were all wearing white golf shirts and khakis on a lawn somewhere, big grins, soft-focus lake and tree behind them.

"How old's your son?" Danielle asked, rising barefoot.

"About to turn seven," he said. There was pride in his voice. "That picture's a few years old." Then he paused, as though having suddenly remembered who she was or, maybe, who he was. "Listen," he said, "should I be worried about something? Because just tell me if I should be." Danielle considered his question. She could see clearly the threads of gray she'd inferred at the bar, and also that he'd missed a spot of stubble around his Adam's apple when he'd last shaved. Had his family left yesterday or just this morning? All his scrupulous duplicity was revealed now, and her father had been the last thing on his mind.

"Oh, I'm nothing to worry about," Danielle said. They stripped their hiking clothes off and got into his shower together. When they got out he put their things in the wash and gave her a robe to wear. It was a man's robe, thankfully, one of his own. She liked feeling small in it. They stood in their robes and watched dusk fall over the island and the docked boats and the ones at anchor and the land on the other side. Buildings on both sides of the harbor lit up their fronts and began to beam lights off of their roofs in an elaborately choreographed sequence. This was the Symphony of Lights, a nightly public spectacle that Danielle had read about it in her guidebook but hadn't yet seen. She thought of the power plant on Lamma, and again of those storefronts in Kowloon. But who was she to condescend, to think she knew what was best, to judge what other people had decided was right for them?

I am Danielle Melman, she thought. Long streaks of color— blue, green, red, purple, white—flashed like lightning across the black water as the show dragged on.

Danielle woke up and slipped quietly out of bed. She used the bathroom—the one in the hallway, so as not to risk disturbing Colin—then stood at the living room window. It was just past dawn. She went back into the master bedroom and woke Colin up. They were making love when his alarm clock went off. He hit the snooze with a flailing hand.

Their clothes had sat in the washer overnight but it would probably be fine, he said, to move them to the dryer now. She asked if he wanted breakfast. He showed her where they kept everything and she cooked them sunny-side-up eggs with turkey bacon and toast. She made their coffee in his Keurig. Did he take sugar? He didn't. Milk? He did. The low-fat stuff or the regular? Either one was fine.

"So what's on tap for today?" she asked.

"Work," he said. "Probably till late since I didn't go in at all yesterday. You?"

"Literally no idea," she said.

"Must be nice."

Danielle, still wearing Colin's robe, got their stuff out of the dryer and spread everything out on the unmade bed. She folded his clothes and laid them on top of the dresser, then gathered her own clothes up into her arms, thinking she would go into the bathroom to change, but when she turned around she saw Colin leaning in the doorframe of the walk-in closet, wearing the same suit he'd been wearing the night they met. He gave her a thin smile but didn't say anything. She understood what he wanted: to see her, all of her, one more time, and then to watch as she disappeared, piece by piece.

The Jewish Cemetery was at 13 Shan Kwong Road in the Happy Valley, about a mile away from the racetrack and the colonial cemetery. An unlocked gate on a steeply sloping residential street—she walked past it twice before she noticed the Star of David in the metalwork. She followed a concrete path between a bamboo construction fence and a day school that was closed for the summer. Behind the school the grounds opened out. There was a durian tree and a stone fountain. Beyond that, the markers and tombs. The heat was brutal but the air hadn't been so clear in weeks. The chopstick buildings shimmered in the high middle distance.

In addition to the usual—name, dates of birth and death, epitaph (many in Hebrew and English, some only in Hebrew, almost none in Chinese)—these markers often listed birthplace. Many of the Jewish dead of Hong Kong, Danielle noticed, hailed from Eastern Europe: Carl Bercovitz, born at Bucharest, 1846, aged 43 years. Pearl Antschel Steinberg, native of Russia, died 3

August 1901, aged 72 years. Pepi Eidelstein, born 25 July 1862 in Brody Austria, died 4 July 1899. Elias Salnicker, Bialostock, Russland, 1862–1898. Mary Bunderoff, Tergu Okna, Rumania, 12 Aug. 1904, aged 31 years. Max Wolff, Kadan Kurland. Carla Dietrich nee Salenicker, wife of Max, mother of Moses Benjamin and Myron Alexander, born in Odessa 3 April 1894, died 22 April 1947.

Rachel Leah Rapoport Rahf, born in Hankow—the rest was in Hebrew, which Danielle couldn't read.

Danielle thought of her grandfather, her father's father, American-born but whose parents (she'd never known them) had come over from Lvov. Her great-grandmother Essie pregnant on the steamer ship, giving birth in a charity hospital or else, more likely, at home. They'd lived in Lower East Side tenements; when their son, Yakov, had come of school age he'd changed his name to Jack, taught himself English, put himself through night school and then law school, bought the building that housed his practice and a brownstone on the southwestern border of Prospect Park. Stan and his sister, Sarah, had grown up in that house, which was later left to them, and they sold it and split the money. Stan married Lynne and they moved to Long Island, then to Westchester, where Danielle had grown up. Between being thrown out of his house and moving to Asia, Stan had rented a walk-up at Ludlow and Hester, right back where the first immigrant Rosses had lived.

Danielle thought about how her life, how all of their lives, would have been different if Essie and her husband, Danielle's great-grandfather—whose name Danielle could no longer recall, if she'd ever known it in the first place—had gotten on a boat bound elsewhere. Or if Essie had died along the way to America, or if she'd stayed put in Lvov. Every choice makes us and remakes us. What's incredible, Danielle thought, is not that we might have been somebody else, or nobody, but rather that despite everything we are somehow still ourselves.

She should send her father a text, she thought: see how his trip was going, if he knew yet when he was coming back. Come to think of it, though, an email might be better—she wouldn't have to be so terse in an email, and he wouldn't feel that text message pressure for an immediate reply. Yes, it would definitely be better to email—which of course she could do with the BlackBerry, but there was a laptop back at the apartment that would be much more comfortable to use. She pictured herself stretched out on her father's couch with the machine in her lap, *Beggars Banquet* tinkling from the small speakers and the sun setting into the bay behind her as she shared her impressions of Lan Kwai Fong, the Jewish cemetery, Lamma Island—all the places she'd been. She imagined him in his Beijing hotel room reading her letter, probably on his BlackBerry, and how the small screen would make whatever she wrote seem much longer than it was. Maybe a text would be better after all—save the stories for when he got back—though of course this still wasn't the place to send it from.

Mrs. Rachel Levy, born in Shanghai, died 2 January 1968, aged 84. Gunner Wilfred Ross, A. A. Regt. Royal Artillery, died at Hong Kong 12 November 1938, aged 20 years. Fanny, dearly beloved wife of S. S. Benjamin, born in London, 1867–1892.

Jacob Ezekiel Dagai: born 1 December 1902, Bombay, India, died 1 August 1999. Samuel Moses Perry: born in Shanghai 29 Feb. 1904, died in Florida U.S.A. 5 Oct. 1981—and yet buried here. In memory of my dear husband, Vladimir Zubitsky, who taught me what real love is, born in Kunelai, Siberia, May 25, 1905, died January 4, 1973. Harry Morgan Weinrebe: born April 1, 1914, Boston, Massachusetts, died March 14, 2000. Anatoly Livshits, no date or place of birth given, died 21 October 2005: Passed away in Shenzhen, alone in this world.

Siegfried Kumur, George Bloch, Adolf Wolepstein, Flora Edgar.

Moselle Gatton, Louisa Anna Green, Elias David Sykes Sassoon.

Danielle dug into the earth with the toe of her sneaker and found a rock. It was smooth and mottled gray-white, smaller than an egg. She placed it atop the Livshits headstone, then made for the shade of the durian tree. The sweet-rot stink of the fruit was almost overpowering but she was glad to be out of the sun. She sat with her back against the trunk and looked out across the sea of graves, then up through the leaves toward the blue apartments anchored in the sky.

GREGORY'S YEAR

March and there's dirty snow humped on the windowsills, still; sidewalk's mucked, sky's been the color of dust for days. He's shaving his head over the bathroom sink, weekly ritual some years now, ever since that monk's tonsure blossomed high in the back. He remembers how the pads of his fingers felt when they first found the smooth patch, warm and soft, and how he thought, Shit no, not gonna be that guy. So instead he's this guy, clean-scalped but boasting a thick beard, well-groomed—hazelnut, he likes to think but would never say. A well-groomed beard is paramount, believes Gregory, who when he meets someone new says "Please, call me Greg" but doesn't mean it. The full name is what he likes, its fine whiff of archaism, bouquet of saints and England, popes and Greece; the two g sounds granting clangorous passage toward the open and humming "ory" with its quick high finish like a young wine, like the inflatable slide you ride to escape from the burning plane. But nobody calls him Gregory except his mother, and he rarely calls her at all. So Greg, then: a higher-up in the lower echelon of a medical copy-writing firm in West Chelsea. Sometimes it seems like science fiction that one blue train line should connect that neighborhood to the part of Bed-Stuy where he's been living for—what is it, two years now? Two years. Merciful Mary. Two years. Fucking hell.

In April he stops at his corner coffee shop for an afternoon latte, asks the barista out on a date. Not only does she say yes, but over Rioja it turns out she doesn't just work at the Grind Shack, she owns it. Used to have another one just like it, successful, in Charlottesville, Virginia, unless she said State College, PA. Anyway she sold that place and bought this one because she wanted to have the experience: city life. Audrey says business is booming but she never imagined she'd hate New York the way she does. She expected an adjustment, sure, but up all night crying? Never. Says she's wolf-whistled at by corner drunks, wants to see a field sometime, may be suffering PTSD from a train grope.

"What can you do?" he says.

"I'm looking for a buyer," she says. He'd meant the question rhetorically—hadn't, in fact, thought it could be taken any other way.

He has these great big bear hands and loves them, favorite thing about himself, easily, the way a double cheeseburger looks a little lost when held in them, or the neck of his old Fender Strat. Proud, too, of the arms on which those hands are mounted: half gift and half result of honest effort (he'd looked into a gym near his office, joined the Y near his place instead). He's in the bathroom, lathering his head. It's May and already most days the mercury's hitting eighty-five by noon. The stripper—one of four strangers he shares this narrow two-story house with—is banging on the door for the second time. She's got her own shaving to take care of, plus mascara, body glitter, diaphragm. She's running late, she says; the car the club sends for her is going to be here any minute. His eyes are red; cheeks round, puffy, hairy, and high. Everything about his job disgusts him. He engineers the jargon that lies the company out of whatever the studies they've done have proven more or less unequivocally. The raw data is enough to keep you up half the night mulching your fingernails, choking back bile and fright. Ergo face puff, ergo eyes. He buys Žižek books by the pound and wine by the gallon. Žižek and Audrey, he feels, are the only people who understand him. Zombies his way through the workweek with a bottomless coffee mug—I'm always on drugs, he thinks at the mirror, always trying to go faster or else slow down, my fingers a beige blur over the beige keyboard, up and down my beige girlfriend; if I were someone else looking at myself at my desk I'd see a slack face bathed in monitor light, dull. He heats the razor by running it under the faucet. He touches the thin hot steel to his head, pulls.

By June Audrey's found her buyer. She's ready to go, but where? He says, "Well, we've both got some money."

She says, "Are you serious? I mean is this us talking serious?"

He says, "I moved to this shit-ass city to become a rock star. Instead I'm an office drone and, increasingly, a raving Communist, only the only times I have time to rave I'm too drunk or too sleepy and the people who need raving at aren't around, or they are but they're holding my leash. Sometimes when I can't sleep I search Craigslist for sublets in Canadian cities. Square footage alone has brought me to the verge of weeping joy." This is the longest monologue he's ever taken in her company. She throws her arms around his wide neck, tilts her pelvis into his hip.

"I want a new guitar," he says. "Acoustic."

Part of the deal for the Grind Shack is Audrey has to help the new owner learn the ropes, so Gregory's alone in Montreal the first few weeks of July. When they Skype he plunks out "Love Minus Zero/No Limit" and can see her in her little digital box, melting for him. And there he is, in his even smaller box inset in the corner of her box, the Ibanez slung across his belly, his sweaty head agleam. Sometimes they let whole minutes pass in silence; he watches her and he watches himself watching her. Audrey in her New York living room, a pale face afloat before a plain gray wall. He takes epic walks around Montreal, up backstreets, down alleys, wherever. If a parade went by he'd probably join it. In a bar near McGill he finds himself knocking back whiskies with a guy who does research on sleep cycles. Guy's going on about fruit flies, the never-ending bitchwork of grant proposals, how it's gonna be when he gets his degree, his own lab, tenure. Guy says he wants to move to New York City. There's a postdoc at Columbia he's got an eye on. Gregory starts to tell him about the old loathed Bed-Stuy share, the way the city stinks in summer. Guy's not saying much anymore and Gregory, worried his frankness has unnerved, swerves toward a different subject.

"Dylan?" says the guy. "Yeah, he's okay, sure, but what about Albert Ayler, Funkadelic, any Dead show from the spring of '74?" Gregory, swaying on his barstool and feeling osmotic, scribbles names and dates on a napkin, offers to get the next round.

The day Audrey's train comes in it starts pouring, doesn't stop for two weeks. They have no idea how to live in a house together. They don't even know where the nearest grocery store is. He's been on an all-takeout diet, trying to figure out whether it's (1) possible and (2) worth it to jam out "China Cat Sunflower" on solo acoustic guitar.

"This isn't working," Audrey says, staring forlorn out their front window at the gray rain veiling the world. Looks back over her shoulder, sees the look on his face, clarifies that she meant Montreal. "Or maybe Canada altogether. We need to get back to the roots of things. Where did you grow up?"

"Indianapolis."

"Okay, forget your roots. What would you say to a cabin in the pines outside of Johnson City?"

Gregory says he's always wanted to explore sweet Dixie. Audrey's sundress makes a blue pool at her feet.

But August is a stupid time to be anywhere. That's what he keeps telling himself to feel better about being here. The cabin has front and back porches he can stand on in the shameless nude. Not bad. But it's forty-five minutes to the nearest strip mall full of chain stores and the rednecks they encounter on their weekly supply trips do not charm him. His faith in Žižek wavers. He thinks the Slovenian has given short shrift to Buddhism; he'd like to investigate for himself but doesn't know where to start. He and Audrey can go a day, days, without speaking, to each other or at all. He can lie down on the floor and listen to Albert Ayler's *Live in Greenwich Village* from start to finish without feeling the least bit restless or opening his eyes even once. Are these things Zen? And if not then what is fucking Zen? Bodies moving past each other through the same hot rooms, pouring cold drinks into jelly jars, throwing steaks in the skillet, flat on their backs in a queen bed, side by side. Sounds all right when you put it that way, but still, something's off.

At the back of the bedroom closet he finds an old math textbook left behind by some former occupant's no doubt underachieving son. He decides Algebra II must be like Buddhism and suggests to Audrey that they seek to master that which they faked their way through in the prehistoric and halcyon days of their respective tenth grades. They work in earnest on problem sets, sneaking glances across the raw scored kitchen table, then check each other's answers. The work gives their lives a grammar and their days a shape. By September they've completed chapter ten, running way ahead of the schedule suggested by the book, though as far as the book knows they are (1) fifteen years old, and (2) taking five other classes besides this one, plus presumably extracurriculars. Audrey says she tried track but wasn't built for it. Ditto honor society, A/V club, chess club, and debate. Gregory played football, had a nickname and everything, until a senior year knee injury reduced him to recording secretary for the local student chapter of the Young Republicans. Their biggest accomplishment had been remembering to show up on Yearbook Picture Day. Three of the six with clip-on ties. Now he's holed up in the woods with this woman, wearing pilled boxers, torn undershirt, unending beard—all three of these articles dried stiff with his own sweat plus Audrey's, having finally mastered that bitch goddess the quadratic equation, and it's like, Who the hell was Jacques Lacan, where the hell on the map is Slovenia, and how could I have ever fallen for this lisping poseur's bad voodoo?

Audrey says her rank-choice vote for the next city is Austin, Texas; Portland, Oregon; Madison, Wisconsin; Portland, Maine. He says, "Baby, when I look in the cracked mirror of this cabin's bathroom what I see is a man who is in the place that is the right place for him."

"'Cause you stopped shaving your head," she says, "or grooming your beard. Your mountain man fantasy's about a half inch deep; see if there are some scissors around we can restore your dignity with—my Lady Bic if it comes to that."

"How will a Lady Bic restore my dignity?"

The night she leaves they have one of those legendary sessions, personal instant classic, a story you'd tell to everyone you knew if you knew how to say it in a way that didn't make you sound retarded: it was exactly the same as always but somehow infinitely better, the best. Then she gets dressed, puts her things in the car, goes, is gone. When her taillights wink out of view he strips down, stands stark on the porch in the crisp October air. It'll be a long walk whenever I leave here, he thinks, and he'd like to write a song about the feeling of that knowledge, an expressive instrumental composition, something soulful and crisp with a touch of melancholy, a kind of bright-eyed fatalism, like John Fahey on *Of Rivers and Religion* or Nathan Salsburg on *Affirmed*. Instead he uses GarageBand to record a twenty-six-minute "Not Fade Away" → "Uncle John's Band" → "Goin' Down the Road Feeling Bad" → reprise of "Not Fade Away." He adds layers of himself doing the harmonies and backups, foot stomps and handclaps, beating forks against the math book and the table and the skillet for a little drum break, emails the result to his brother as the first sunbeams cut through the pines. His brother writes back an hour later: "If you need a place to crash you can say so."

Kevin is five years younger, has a wife, lives in Philly, which Gregory quickly comes to recognize is a provincial shithole filled with ugly people uninterested in traffic laws or any other form of etiquette or self-preservation. Regaining his urban anomie is like physical therapy, but faster and more rewarding. He grows a goatee but not a soul patch. By the end of November he's got his brother reading Žižek, who makes glorious apocalyptic sense again, and Kevin's got him into the whole slow-food thing. Kevin's become this genius chef, apparently, side benefit of his status as one of the long-term unemployed. The brothers spend their time talking revolution, crimping piecrusts, slow-cooking brisket, brining turkey, baking bread from scratch. The first time his dough rises Gregory is unashamed to shed a tear, indeed, rather wishes he would have broken wholly down.

Sounds very cleansing, freeing, to be emptied out, presumably as prelude to some experience of renewal, anyway refill. He bites into an onion as though it were a Honeycrisp, but the moment seems to have passed.

The wife, his sister-in-law, is Nancy. At night when she comes home from her job in the archives at a university art museum they sit in the living room and sing their favorite songs together, a bottle of rye going around the circle like a looped video clip while they debate whether their cover of "Promised Land" is a Dead cover or a Chuck Berry cover since the Dead were covering Berry in the first place but the Dead version is the only one they've ever heard. Nancy suggests they YouTube the original—a Gordian solution, granted, but one that seems to Gregory a pinhole glimpse into the sorry heart of the contemporary world. When she teasingly leans toward his MacBook they have words. His brother, an untalented drinker, is curled up on the couch, head in hands.

Kevin and Nancy cajole Gregory to fly back to Indianapolis with them for Christmas. Their father is straight John Birch these days, but weirdly, this doesn't ruin the visit. Gregory realizes that apart from a few particulars about immigration and Jewish people, their beliefs are basically aligned: the system is both rigged and rotten, the economy is one continuous act of fraud, anyone wearing a tie on the TV has already been bought and sold. They both voted for Obama, now feel betrayed. Two days before New Year's, in the parking lot of Harris Teeter, he runs into Kara, a girl from his high school, a B-lister from the old vanished Hollywood of his adolescent porn dreams, hardly worse for a decade's wear, he's got to say; in fact she's held up better than a lot of the old A-list, if Facebook's any way to judge. He's on his way out of the store and she's on her way in. "Gregory?" she says. "Is that you? Oh em gee, I'd heard you were in New York."

They catch up while his twelve-pack of Beast Ice sweats through its paper box. She's home for the holidays like he is, says she lives in Detroit now, is separated from her terminally alcoholic husband, is a painter in roughly the same sense that he's a rock star. "You should come visit sometime," she says. After a few weeks of increasingly familiar emails, he does—in January no less. If he lived here, he decides, he'd be in love with her in three months, which, he further muses, is probably about when she'll be ready to give some kind of rebound thing a try. Back in Philly he buys a '93 Camry, throws his guitar in the trunk, big hugs for his brother and sister-in-law. "Your devotion," he says, "will not be forgotten. You are granted title to great mansions in the sky." He hitches up his pants. They're loose. You wouldn't believe the difference fresh, organic, homemade food makes. It was Philly itself that taught him this, as much as his brother. Yellow drip cheese, half-priced buffalo wings, smeary death. No thanks.

Lease on the Detroit apartment starts February 15. A whole floor to himself for what his shoe-box room cost in that Bed-Stuy share. It's time to work again so he gets into a gig doctoring white-collar résumés, still despicable in its way but less categorically or directly so, and he can do it from home. He takes long drives in his car whenever he feels like it, soaks up such beauty and desolation as Detroit abides—in a month or two when spring returns many of these empty white lots will be blooming fields, Audrey's rural-urban dream realized, but he doesn't write her to tell her about it. She must have other dreams now.

He picks Kara up from work, cooks her dinner whenever she'll let him, but it's not time for the next step yet and both of them know it, which somehow makes everything easier rather than fraught like you might expect. What is expectation, anyway? A fantasy. A shot in the dark. A wish. What is anything? Who was this man Chesterton whose bons mots Žižek is always pinching? What would it have been like to have lived one of the lives of the saints? Gregory makes flank steak with raspberry-chipotle marinade, fingerling potatoes au gratin. Salmon and asparagus with Israeli couscous. Apple cobbler, peach pie. He pulls the guitar off its stand while the dishes soak, plinks around to get himself loose and in tune. Kara's on the love seat, legs tucked up. He clears his throat, grins shyly, launches into his new favorite cover, an old country blues—Garcia loved it— called "Sitting on Top of the World."

AUTHOR'S NOTE

"Flings" is, among other things, in loose homage to Virginia Woolf's *The Waves*.

In "A Night Out," Candi's recurring dream is of Paul Klee's *Ghost Chamber with the Tall Door*.

"Adon Olam" owes a debt—and perhaps an apology—to Gershom Scholem's *On the Mystical Shape of the Godhead*.

"Mike's Song" is a quasi-sequel to a story called "The New Life," which appears in my first collection. The concert the Becksteins attend is a real historical event, used here fictitiously but true to the set list as performed. My sister, Melanie, went with me when nobody else would, and we had a better time than Mike did—even though our seats were a lot worse.

"Carol, Alone" and "The Happy Valley" both make use of my maternal family history. My grandparents Lorelei and Jack Starkman and my great-aunt Ellen Greenberg were patient with my questions, generous with their answers, and will please forgive all omissions, distortions, and honest mistakes. I would also like to acknowledge Lord Lawrence Kadoorie's letter of February 6, 1979 ("The Kadoorie Memoir"), Dennis A. Leventhal's article "The Jewish Community of Hong Kong: An Introduction," and Ken Nicolson's book *The Happy Valley: A History and Tour of the Hong Kong Cemetery*, which mentions the Jewish cemetery only in passing, but is nonetheless the text that alerted me to its existence. And I wouldn't have been in Hong Kong in the first place if not for the love and hospitality of the Goldners: Caryn, Andrew, Ava Grace, and Lillian Jade.

ACKNOWLEDGMENTS

Thank you to the editors of the journals, magazines, and websites where several of these stories first appeared.

For steadfast love and friendship, close readings, saintly patience, stiff drinks, and otherwise Coming Through, my boundless gratitude is offered to Noah Ballard, Mary Beth Constant, Elliott David, Mark Doten, Dan Guy Fowlkes, Caryn & Andrew Goldner, Gregory Henry, Jodie Mack, Peter Masiak, Cal Morgan, Alec Niedenthal, Amanda Peters, Suzanne Rindell, Jarrett Rosenblatt, Michael Signorelli, Emma Sweeney, Eva Talmadge, Maggie Tuttle, and Adam Wilson; my parents and sister; all the Taylors and Bullocks;

and Jeremy Schmall—whose Giant goes with him wherever he goes;

Joshua Cohen—for guidance, indulgence, and translations from the Hebrew;

Amanda Bullock—for Everything, all the time.

ABOUT THE AUTHOR

JUSTIN TAYLOR is the author of the story collection *Everything Here Is the Best Thing Ever* and the novel *The Gospel of Anarchy*. He lives in Portland, Oregon.

BOOKS BY JUSTIN TAYLOR

FLINGS
Stories

Available in Paperback and eBook

"Hilarious and heartbreaking . . . [Captures] all the confusion, repressed aggression, and misplaced acceptance of growing up in the nineties and becoming a young adult in the twenty-first century."

—Andrew Jimenez, *The Paris Review*

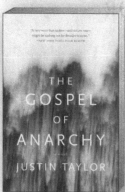

THE GOSPEL OF ANARCHY
A Novel

Available in Paperback and eBook

"Remember this name: Justin Taylor. You will hear it again. He is audacious, intelligently literate and fizzing with potential."

—*Miami Herald*

EVERYTHING HERE IS THE BEST THING EVER
Stories

Available in Paperback and eBook

"Justin Taylor is a master of the modern snapshot."

—*Los Angeles Times*